SACRIFICE RETURNED

I. SATAN

TM

Nemean Press
First Conquer Thyself
PRIMO EVINCO TE

Richard L. Matteoli
Sacrifice Returned

2nd Edition

E-ISBN: 978-1-943347-46-9
Soft Cover ISBN: 978-1-943347-47-6
Hard Cover ISBN: 978-1-943347-48-3

Images:
Front: *The Sacrifice of Abraham*, Andrea del Sarto, 1486-1530
Back: *Satan*, Gustav Dore, from Milton's "Paradise Lost," c. 1866
Back: Pitt-Rivers Egyptian ritual flint knife, British Museum

Bibliography:
Chad Brand, Charles Draper, Archie England, General Editors, *Holman Illustrated Bible Dictionary*, Holman Bible Publishers, 2005.

Cooper, JD, *Dictionary of Symbolic & Mythological Animals*, Thorsons, 1995.

Acknowledgement: John J. Whitworth

CONTENTS

DEATH

    I, Satan, am and in the immediate presence of the Spirit most Holy intertwined as One with the Most Almighty.

    The most Holy-Almighty has given me a vision. My duty is to pass that vision on to you.

    The honor to do so is a blessing. The privilege is overwhelming. This mission: my faithful existence.

    I was sent to roam the four corners of the earth and document what you have done with the things you take from the seas of the social.

    Upon my return and after my report is when this vision was given me, for you.

    Hear well: listen carefully: read completely: remember fully. You are to meet your future.

    The sky is completely bright and golden as the glorious roof of all the heavens above. It sparkles from every region and in each space between.

    This sky's vastness, the expanse, shows infinity itself.

    You see a Rider atop a formidable white horse.

    This rider flashes back and forth dressed and colored first in white, and then black encompasses as total emptiness within.

White is the most Holy-Almighty's truthfulness. Black tells your evil ways and heart's dark future.

Rider holds a bow and wears a crown.

Rider and horse appear to be facing aside, but intent is solely focused on you.

They turn and face you directly.

This horse starts its approach slowly.

With Rider in white you hear a booming voice of thunder ask: "Do you believe in God."

When echoes pass, follows like the rushing of all waters: "I believe in God."

This horse changes its gait a little quicker, slowly in a trot becoming faster and faster progressing toward you.

Feverish hoof beats ascend louder and louder as if flint stomping your sacrificial stones.

At the proper moment Rider reaches back grabbing arrows from their quiver.

Rider then shoots silver arrows that do not miss.

Immediately all existence become nothingness.

No song in your heart; no music in your soul.

Then a little light slowly, slowly, ever so slowly becomes exponentially larger. It ends with a flash as the whole screen of your being turns bright light.

Finally, your nothingness in a vacuum of only you: into multitudes screaming with the infant's cry.

Alone, in total anguished separateness. And no one will hear you beseech.

Satan says, "Do not ask for your sacrifice's return; it's an insult. The most Holy-Almighty sends men to mete retribution. Repent or eternally die."

LIFE

"I, Satan, report your behavior before the most Holy-Almighty. You do what you do, and like it.

Your myths changed me in many ways. Those changes are your self-deceit. It is you who make you think the way you think – even toward me.

Repent or you will surely pass into nothingness never forever experiencing the radiance of the most Holy-Almighty!"

All things known, still yet unknown and those things that will come to you are before me encircling as objects for this vision given by the Holy-Almighty has gifted you brought by me.

These objects in constant whirling motion are embodied as if real to be reached for and grasped, then given to your perception.

Everywhere my reach extended just far enough. But reaching could not capture. These images filtered spritely easily through.

Yet a special tingle was felt particular to each object. The purpose of their meaning passed for me to tell.

You think you will survive the trial heaven is sending. No. You will perish. The trial is one, during the same mythic moment for all who you make suffer.

Blessings have been promised. Whatever your blessings were now or to be, are now denied.

Through your free will, the choices you made determine where you go when I am sent to observe the harvest of your soul.

Supplicating implorement in confession and bribing through atonement falls on deaf ears.

Standing on false words and improper deeds to create a stairway to paradise has and never will exist.

Your words and deeds are forever unforgivable in the eyes of the most Holy, thus with the Most Almighty.

You prosecute yourself.

No one can defend you and your lie.

You will forever not even be a continued fading sound or whispering echo from the gnashing of your teeth in indiscernible screams.

You will be less than a speck of sand with the multitude in agony throughout time everlasting.

Man is born from woman. She is Nature. Mas is the Servant of Nature. Her ethos is Nature to Action. His ethos is Action to Nature.

His action is Servancy: the willing performance in duty to maintain life's necessities. Life is a series of oppositions. Without him she is overwhelmed.

But, her bringing a bonding may be anathema.

Existence consists of endless cycles including: minutes of the hour, hours in a day and days of a year.

Cycles belong to the seasons, celestial rotations. For humanity the most important cycle is earth's moon.

The cycle of life, as all cycles meant to be, turns like a wheel. There are many wheels, each belonging to one of the minions of living creatures from nature. At times they wheels seem as if syncrotizing.

Some wheels of life are large, some small, and there are all sizes and types in between.

Where wheels first rest, there is a starting point on the ground, and a starting point on the wheel.

With first movement the wheel of life forever leaves, never to return.

Thus: Life begins its journey with a spot of ground's residue in its tread.

The wheel's center is its hub. The hub is inner most to the wheel's existence. It is the structure from which all other parts extend outward as well as inwardly attached.

This hub is as the body's mind. It harbors your unknowing. It is the port in your vast inner sea that anchors and moors activity.

What is done to the hub determines the wheel's direction. The hub of your life truly affects you.

You made a god who says to bleed like you, and pass this down through the generations.

So, you killed this man and let him live.

His calling announced by pure waters now makes him the one to roam the earth as not live.

He understands you, what you do not know of yourself. It is your way. It is your game.

He lives among you unnoticed. You will not perceive him asocial.

He does not outwardly rebel. You will not deem him overly antisocial.

He will not join you.

He is coming for you.

When he comes, you will not know his hunting began – for you so instantly final.

He unraveled the web of your deceit.

This man is now the spider, and you the fly.

First, he will find you through quiet observation. To see what you do in your secret open circles

He is doing that now.

He discovered what you made for yourself. He documents what you do for his studied pursuing.

His function is the spark of your all-consuming apocalyptic fire,

The tinder you prepared for yourself will engulf you during time everlasting. Unforgivable.

This man is now the cat, and you the mouse.

This vision came to me in an instant.

It is passed to you in dire warning.

Sear it forever in your heart's memory.

Without question your ending comes.

The choice of your ending is at hand.

Allow yourself life everlasting.

He lives. Your curse now comes through this one allowed.

Call him – *Sanguineri*.

His words by you sending him living death are: "I am your antichrist because you were my antichrist.

CONCEPTION

"I, Sanguineri, am in your presence. Yet, personally, I am at a distance. Each pulsating heart beat deep in your chest brings me a footstep closer.

I traveled to the threshold before the door I will open and pass into your life.

You I will touch. Put your affairs in order.

I am not to be copied. The mission is not yours. I am the professional. Admire the art of my being, as your future unfolds.

A whippoorwill is present for its song's familiar mourning call, because it is one with nature.

My journey begins."

"I, Satan, say it started for him in the womb at beginning existence. In his first beginning no vision, no touch, no sound and no smell; not even tasting.

Nothing was present but a deep unconscious primal being of the self. It was one expansive sense of being engulfed in the Holiest of spirit's existence.

A total surrounding, an endless floating, contained, by the waters of the great mother: This awesome mother of all nature.

Only her aura spoke to him who she was forming. The most Holy spirit gave him her direction.

11

Laid before him was the prescription of his future. There was no choice but to accept, take, obey – only until revenge.

It is his future of sorrows.

This direction is a part of your future too.

You take away happiness, total bliss.

Your decision in consequence caused your future to be everlasting oblivion.

You belong to generations in perdition.

Acts of a person, or peoples, through exercise of free will have unalterable effects on the predestination of others toward the good as well as the bad.

But in certain situations, the mirror does not reflect truly.

Faith is yours to come to terms with. It is a believing not an empirical proving.

Faith is a sense deep inside. The something that inherently tells you: "It is so."

Faith may very well determine your choices. Choices you make in life are important especially when Sanguineri comes to meet you.

Little faith is required for you to know on that day he most certainly will come into your presence.

It is deemed so by the most Holy-Almighty.

Pay close attention to your beating heart within. Sense the coursing of your blood as it flows.

The blood feeds you. It keeps you warm. It brings life into the pit of your stomach which will bring a lump caught in your throat.

This blood knows. It worries. It chills the spine and tingles the hairs on the back of your neck.

Faith determiners belief. Belief determines faith.

Come to terms with the actions you have taken from misguided faith in deifying yourself."

Sanguineri will tell you with a warning his life's mission to the windowsill of your soul.

His tortured whispers say unto you:

"Recognize you are not masters of someone else's tent. Despite your best intentions, you must, by the nature of things, humiliate us to control us.

You feel men are of no importance. What counts is who is in control. You now are the hunted.

Your acts put in your mind as if you are the most Holy-Almighty.

There is jo forgiveness without change.

Forgiveness is determined by the most Holy-Almighty; not mine or with the duty given me.

My obligation to this mission given began thusly."

The Pacific Ocean is observed flying southward into San Francisco. It is best seen when sitting on a right sided window seat.

Patterns of steep sea cliffs mixed with rocky shores and sandy beaches illustrate nature's variation.

In springtime commercial flower gardens occasionally appear. The western landscape is mapped with various shades of green.

This journey during summer ocean view varies little. The landscape matures tarnished brown prepared to return to earthly sod. Summer below cyclically recounts the season of grass has passed.

All is dried readied for the tinder. Brittle grass reminds such is the transitory nature of the cycle of life.

Observation. Attention to detail.

Approach was long ago determined.

The Golden Gate Bridge appears below. Bypassing ever moving San Francisco is over the abandoned stone prison on Alcatraz Island.

Oakland Bay Bridge connected in its middle by closed Treasure Island Naval Base still harbors private ships and yachts.

Such is life, passing every action taken well thought out or not considered at all.

After the craziness of a California drive, respite is reached in Fisherman's Wharf.

Always first is time to reflect at the moored Pampanito. This refurbished submarine silently and slightly aways with moving tides.

All is not as things appear. A Boat as this sank an unmarked Japanese transport carrying Prisoners of War.

Many Allied personnel were killed.

But not all friendly fire is unintentional.

Such a killing was not the complete fault of the submarine's Captain and crew. Larger fault belongs to those whom hid the truth the vessel carried those doomed soldiers, sailors and Marines.

So, it is the same with Shepherds of people, in whatever chosen profession where power, control and authority reside.

Truly, they will be held more responsible when their judgment day arrives upon my unannounced introduction.

The lull.

After my recurring reminder, a short meander takes me to the outside market filled with smells of fresh seafood, especially crab.

This area is roofed creating a walkway in front of the main building housing other special businesses.

A taste must be taken and container put in the trash.

Behind the many little shops is a fisherman's legacy passed down. Alioto's Restaurant is a place of both peace and celebration.

In the back one can sit and see little ships that harvest the ocean. Here are special times for quiet reflection of past aspirations, for hopeful things to come that was in the end sought in vain.

Even here can be seen truth life is always in motion with change, especially when seals make their presence dominant as they rest on wooden walkways outlining the slips.

For a man in my trained and experienced profession it is best to sit with my back against a wall, facing outside observing all surroundings.

People must be studied especially when special events are set to evolve.

For the moment, pleasant solace reaches in touching the hearts from families and lovers dining.

A man thin and balding sits nearby reminds me of times before, as if he has importance to convey.

Notice was made, acknowledgment secured. The rest passed into history.

Before the storm.

Golden Gate Park is stately with original flora. Later plantings intersperse eucalyptus, pines, cedars and other varietals.

Nature is vibrant through every season. Whether a warm day under the sun, rainy overcast, or blanketed in cool misty fog there are always moments capturing you in awe of Holy creation, as are we a part of and in it.

The Children's Playground is the oldest of its type in the United States. Its carousel placed eastwardly still goes round and round for each successive generation. It is fitting for young to be towards the rising sun as dawn of a new day, life itself.

On the western side close to the ocean tulips are planted by windmills originally used to bring fresh water to nourish the park. And the sacrifice thirst not knowing why.

Nature's flora is illustrated and contained in the Conservatory of Flowers, Strybing Arboretum and Botanical Gardens. They display world biodiversity created from the spirit most Holy, planted by the Most Almighty. Just as so are we.

Flowers resonate blooming as children at play during life's beginnings.

The Music concourse, surrounded by cultural attractions, with fountains and statues observing, sings praises for our Holy existence.

The climate is such every month has its own special song.

As we grow other interests develop absorbed in the course of a way of life. Learning life and how lived in the past are important in humanity's forward movement.

The Academy of Sciences houses the Steinhart Aquarium, Morrison Planetarium as well as exhibiting world geology and fauna. The De Young Museum showcases the past so we may contemplate the present and look to the future.

On designed North Spreckels Lake, model yachts sail. It is paved completely along the edges. Yet one area is a grassy ramp so ducklings come and go safely.

In the center of Golden Gate Park slightly south is another lake. Stow Lake surrounds an island called Strawberry Hill for those more active. People use rowboats, pedalboats even electric powered boats to share enjoyable days.

Loons of lakes half a continent away give their plaintiff call for things unfolding, for they too are one in all nature with their own special song.

Between Stow Lake and the Asian Art Museum is the five-acre Japanese Tea Garden. It is said to be the birthplace of the fortune cookie that always given at the end of a meal in American Chinese restaurants.

Buddha is present in quiet contemplation as if with a halo gracing his head.

A Tea House in the lush landscape serves cuisine while the five roofed Pagoda is by the Temple Gate. There is a Zen Garden with stone waterfall and a stone bed river surrounding a tiny island.

A carved stone water basin is present in the shape of a boat.

Along the Tea Garden's pathways is the remarkable Drum Bridge arching over the waterway.

Further down is the Long Bridge.

In the waterway's little ponds are multi-colored koi. Within is the Lantern of Peace.

I know my Killing Fields and Lines of Sight. It is time for business. Now I am your Sacrifice Returned. Me who you took my nature never to sense or enjoy.

The maiden is jogging along one of many pathways in Golden Gate Park. It is during day's end, the sun dipping below the ocean waters.

Shadows grow around tree pillars engulfing shrub houses planted between.

The cap on her head with visor at front has a space in the back for her hair to pass through. Her hair is as long train that follows a royal priestess's robe.

On her warm sweater is a beginning New Moon with the Big dipper's stars as if a gold chalice holding her misbegotten symbol of life through mock taking.

Turning the winding route she simply stumbled and fell.

No sound except a puff from the wind.

This is duly recorded with token left close beside; yet still distant.

Locations like the San Francisco Bay Area are conducive to hunting.

Coldest summers come and go daily.

Winter presents vast variation.

It is not unusual to dress prepared for a quick changing weather.

A knapsack can carry many personal things.

You should visit Golden Gate Park once in your life. Don't wait. You never know.

Flying back, north from San Francisco to Seattle, the Sierra Nevada mountains then the Cascades are seen sitting on the likewise right sided window seat.

Each time distant outlines appear the same. Yet beyond our perceptions as oceans erode coast lines, so too the slow mountain erosion.

During autumn, orchards, vineyards, and fields of grain are harvested while first winter grasses are turning landscapes like a thin green sheet over nature's Mother Earth. But our sacrificed had their nature taken.

During winter the high mountains are covered with snow. Inhabitants below hope enough water to fill lakes and manmade irrigation facilities work for next year's crops.

Here nature gives sustenance for her creation.

Life ebbs away. How will you end? By revenge?

A sacrificial scar never heals; it's but a blasphemous replacement.

The day after Sanguineri returned to Seattle. It was time recheck terrain and reconnaissance.

He joined people getting on Seattle's South Lake Union Trolly. Some residents affectionally call it: Riding the SLUT.

A few bold souls wear clothes announcing the trolly's name reminding us of life's situations.

This evening a woman is visiting the Asian displays in Volunteer Park meandering while shopping.

It is raining as usual during this time of year.

In rain people walk protectively head down not noticing surroundings.

On one occasion she took off her coat and is wearing a scarlet sweater with an embroidered full white moon surrounded by twelve tiny stars.

These are secret messages to a possible few they may incidentally pass.

Her window shopping is taking forever. Most is for conversation. When finished it is raining very hard.

She is a woman walking alone.

He walked toward her with umbrella open as a slightly lame man in trench coat and hat. Using short shuffling steps he gave her wide lead-way, by politely moving to the outside of the sidewalk.

They pass. He drops her token on the sidewalk.

At the corner he turned and she instantly fell.

Quickley rounding the corner he moved normal away from the site.

Seattle's Space Needle is seen where the World's Fair was once held. The Log Book is filled. One more duly recorded entry is made. Next the old woman.

This old grey-haired woman was dressed in a purple-colored blouse with a blood red moon front center. Long slacks were loose and baggy.

Her slightly wide brimmed hat worn was a tiara that came crashing down from the pedestal of her head.

Our meeting was an instant close, to Forest Park's Planetarium.

Her heart's blossoms were faded, wilted in body and mind. The blood she spilled kept her focused and insatiable.

She no longer gives direction to false sacred ways, her chosen profession. The one who sacrifices.

Value of such is worth less than anything in her coin purse she everywhere carried.

This old woman's widow mite stored safely in her misbegotten heart carried improper images holding meaningless value.

Her first rest expressed quandary in wonder, surprise, though she could not see the token given. Her glassy eyes gaze, but see nothing.

Realization was too late in choices she made. Her blood power held inside was sin in blood taking.

Her eclipsed moon completed its waning.

The road to finality has now been taken.

She now takes her road to perdition.

The time of judgment for all.

The most Holy-Almighty demanded my visit.

It is recorded elsewhere in view of the St. Louis Arch by the balding man as he sits reading the news.

The screech owl, a creature of the night, continents away, mourns the loss of another one of her offspring.

Sanguineri in whispering voice reminds, "We all began as something else. Such change is hard to accept. Children have little need to deceive others."

Sanguineri's punishing ecstasy was in his first seeds for vengeance. Retribution cast on targets are from innocent victims from bitter waters was cast.

These acts were penetrating blooding events. Blood for blood.

These events moved to the mindless cave from which all their bitter waters ooze forth and do eventually, in return, ebb back to drown them in bitterness.

These waters do not support true life and are as dry as exposed whitened bones.

Whether you are young, middle aged or ancient in days, playing dark devious game of blasphemous actions are only repetitions that became your reality.

These actions come in the ages of Blood Venus Rising and there they are maintained throughout all the short and long-term cycles of the stars in the heavens.

The seed of your destruction began its journey. This seed's senses are developed. They are warning:

Do not hear. Listen!

Do not see. Envision!

Do not touch. Feel!

Do not smell. Decipher!

Do not taste. Absorb!

"I, Satan, accuse you of taking your darkened and hardened hearts to the wondrous creation of life given you as a gift by the one most Holy-Almighty.

This gift is not yours to play evil with.

You create violence bringing violent acts into your families, communities and outward into all the places you reside.

Yet you cry, point fingers and blame others all in projective deflection."

BIRTH

Good fortune to calamity is called fate by some. In part, this may be true instance.

Most often than not, choice is ours to make. Why we choose may be implanted early within us. Choice is decision whether conscious or not.

Fate and predestination are connected, as if an act from choice we make we say is through predestination. Acting on our choices creates a fate and we own it.

Then the created fate becomes excused predestination as if destiny itself.

Impulse becomes uncontrollable excuse.

Excuses are part of your character. So, legacy will be in your most certain final judgment.

Boston is a fine example of human endeavor digging a hole at other people's expense.

Promises made with grand assurance.

Yet reality in hearts known is the price taken is a grave tom those who pay the unfair toll up front.

And life moves forward forgetting, not caring.

Once a bargain is struck, taking becomes a demand then a presumed right in the taker's obsession.

Sometimes there's birthed a different death in the taking.

The death given leaves but a pittance for the taken, a false death of demanded existence remaining.

But their sacrifice's revenge will be re-born life resurrected.

Boston's Holy Family Hospital is a stately institutional building.

Its entrance has a semi-circular driveway with doors protected by a column supported breezeway.

Across the entrance a hedge shaped as a new moon with evergreen aside looms majestically silent.

There is a lack of compassion.

The name Holy Family is fitting for a hospital such as this. Deep within is the womb birthing center.

Promise in family is clothed with flowered expressions form the sacred event made given by the most Holy-Almighty.

Accountability is tattered.

The birthing center accommodates mother with a family centered area where each mother has a private bath and shower.

A comprehensive parenting education program on caring for new arrivals is included.

Respect is differential.

There is a sleeper chair for a family member to be by the mother.

So too, are a special intensive care nursery for newborns and a regular nursery to view fresh arrivals.

Board Certified excellence is selective.

Thus, Sanguineri as if a newborn ghost reminds, "Our beginning is a very delicate time."

The newborn is lethargic with blank staring eyes half closed being returned from his sacrifice and placed in his mother's arms.

This baby looks as if he tried to fight and has lost. His blood moon sacrifice now complete.

All he was doing was vain attempts to survive the scrambling power surge that cursed in his brain.

Shock has set in.

Nurse Luna tries to assure the neonate just arrived that, "It's OK, you'll come out of it like the brave little man you are. Your whole life is ahead of you."

After the mother had taken her newborn, Luna also assured her by giving standard instructions for proper care of her newborn along with a few pieces of associated medical literature.

Sanguineri's newly birthed voice states the proper perspective instructing, "Often from the start, appropriate care is doing nothing at all. Remember, as so in history, you and yours have drawn first blood."

Afterward Nurse Luna walks quickly toward and into the nursing bay station.

She put the newborn's chart in its slot of a file holder attached to the wall and approaches other nurses on the shift.

Luna joyfully, "These studies about suicide correlating to the types of birth complications and general violence are interesting. It's a good thing they don't remember, or else we'll be creating a bunch of serial killers."

A second nurse looking down and making notes, Alessandra, states, "We are."

Alessandra, now looks up and gives Nurse Luna an unapproving look.

After pausing, Allesandra admonishes, "Your surgery station is your altar. They are your sacrifices."

Luna snidely retorts, "Sandra, you're such a drag. It can be conditioned to behave the way we want. Nurture over Nature."

Luna turns to face another nurse, Cybele.

Cybele defending Luna emphatically states, "Sandra, lighten up. We have a right to demand it."

Alessandra, "No – you don't. It is a deliberate difference."

Luna ignores Alessandra while taking her timecard and punches out.

Excitedly Luna tells Cybele, "Date tonight."

Cybele giggling says, "Chased him until he caught you. Hook's in. Have fun."

Luna replies to Cybele "More than twenty minutes late. Had a bleeder. Good thing parents don't know how often this happens."

Luna starts to leave.

Cybele teases Luna, "Skip your hair. He's already memorized you."

Luna leaves.

A fourth nurse at the nursing station, Jenny, looks up at Allesandra, "I hope they will learn the subtle difference between holding a hand and chaining a soul."

Alessandra, "She's not going to keep him. He'll give up. She's all confused because he has a hard time talking. He must be realizing the prize is not worth the price."

Then Alessandra reflects, "If she gets her way, he'll hate her forever and still not talk."

Jenny replies, "Heard you got your notice for standing your ground not assisting for that. Stay positive."

Alessandra, "Thanks, my destiny is elsewhere."

Jenny, "They glorify themselves This is much more than healthy self-esteem. One day these pretty ones will realize that men truly desire someone who will be supportive and give them peace."

Alessandra, "Takers find givers because they find them weak. They use them up not realizing love is the greatest strength. Even if with someone, they'll grow old with a little dog. If alone, they'll wind up with a cat."

Jenny, "Shunning is the Bible's way of saying – Ignore the Bitch."

Luna is bubbly in anticipation of her date.

In her exuberance she hurries weaving through the hospital's corridors alone in her mind.

She is so wrapped up it can be said she was ignoring other staff members walking this way and that.

Close to the exit, as the corridor opens into the main lobby, two Nuns approach ever so silently strolling in watchful interest.

From a distance, Luna looking concerned and confused greeted the nuns.

At the end of their greetings one nun pats Luna on the shoulder and then the two nuns turn away.

Luna continues on her way with a bouncier happier walk along with a smile after what appears to have been some kind of nun's affirmations.

There are no sounds from Luna's footsteps. She is in nursing shoes.

Outside the hospital exit Luna takes out her ever so ready cell phone and dials her boyfriend to tell him she is running late.

Luna gleefully hops down the step to the driveway in front of the hospitals entrance.

She starts to her car as if a schoolgirl skipping.

In this Boston early evening winter chill, she could only think about her happiness and future.

All is now and forever be under her control.

As Luna is walking a figure in shadows next to the shrubs lining the perimeter in the hospital parking lot watches.

The person in silent motion is dressed in dark warm clothing.

Only shoes can be seen beyond the long overcoat. They are wrapped. These steps are light and delicate as a leopard stalking.

All that is heard is the light crunching sound of snow that lightly covers the few remaining leaves laying on the grass below.

Approaching close enough, Luna unlocks her car with a remote, opens the door and sits down putting her purse on the passenger seat.

Before she could close the door Luna flinches to relaxation.

There were two puffs of sounds from the shooting. The weapon had a noise suppressor.

The gun was hidden in a bag not to be seen and this bag caught its spent ejected shell casings.

Luna simply slumps toward the passenger side over her purse with nothing else to see, say or demand.

The sweet happy life Luna thought was ahead abruptly ended as the newborn's tortured beginning is just starting in living death.

Sanguineri tosses a paper bag where Luna has now slid headfirst down to the passenger side floor.

It is all well and fitting for this to be so.

Sanguineri's child-like whisper speaks, "We simply never know why this, our sacrifice, is demanded with so many reasons. I am quite certain these crimes will never be purged away but with blood."

This man of blood revenge simply walks away into the shadows of the early night satisfied this part of his mission has been successfully accomplished and recorded.

He thinks the song Respect, not ever given the child.

The way of Boston's Caritas Christi, picking and choosing a Way of the Living by sacrifice in mayhem, angers the most Holy-Almighty.

So, it has been decreed that Sanguineri was given the privilege to touch Luna's final sensing.

As he fades into the night after the faded life of lady nurse Luna, he will also fade into the mass of humanity to touch you.

The crime scene of Luna's sweet departure is so typical that one may surmise the familiarity.

It is as if every profession's protocols are rituals unto themselves. This is true whether or not the protocol is medicine bringing in life

And there is protocol in criminal medicine taking a life through a mock-death blood ritual where an existence is killed to be replaced with a lesser existence.

Yellow tape is wrapped around this once nurse's car with reclining body inside.

There are three local police cars side by side forming a line on one side of the parking lot's crime scene, while two state cars are placed on the opposite end.

All vehicles have their lights silently flashing.

An ambulance is present with two attendants standing by with a gurney for its passenger Luna.

And, a tow truck is waiting.

All vehicles are positioned just outside the taped off occasion.

The coroner's office has still not arrived.

Some uniformed police stand vigil while others look outside the taped perimeter hunting for hopeful clues.

Far away are onlookers to Luna's solemn scene. Most are hospital staff and others.

Almost all keep silent observance whereas a few small groups surmise questions and answers to Luna's blessed event.

Up close a crime scene photographer takes pictures with partner documenting.

With efficiency at the crime scene, a standard unmarked police sedan arrived after slowly weaving its way through the inquisitive human obstacles.

It parks behind the three local police cars with engines still running.

An older man drives and first to get out. He is nicely dressed in trench coat with collar up. On his head a black fedora sporting a small a small red feather is neatly placed in its band.

Before shutting the car's door, he leans back in and says tauntingly to his partner, "Leo, Wakey-Wakey time."

The man in the passenger seat slouches with his head against the window trying to get a few more seconds of sleep.

He's as if in a cocoon wrapped snug and toasty in a Navy p-coat and black cold weather knit cap cover on his head.

As he painfully starts to exit the sedan it becomes obvious, he is much younger than the driver.

Leo is unshaven with messy regulation military haircut.

With a tired look Leo says, "Dominic, this better be worth waking me up for. Jeez, you can do this without me."

Dominic replies, "I'm glad you appreciate my sense of humor, but it really doesn't matter."

Walking to Leo's side of the car Dominic continues, "You're working too much. Concentrate on your studies. You need to graduate."

Leo replies, "Chief Kenny keeps giving me more and more. It's constant and never ending."

Leo then taunts back at Dominic, "Yeah, and I see you appreciate my social appropriateness."

Dominic reaches Leo. He slaps upturned palm and jokingly continues, "Everyone is in such awe."

The evening became colder. Breaths can now be seen when people exhale.

So too the lined police cars exhausts are creating a visible vapor that the two pass through in eerie silence.

Their eyes are transfixed walking straight forward toward Luna's death door.

As they walk uniformly as friends often do, to the crime scene both take out a pen and notebook.

Reaching the yellow taped off crime scene, they show their badges to the uniformed policeman on the perimeter.

Officer Jackson, crime scene officer in charge smiles while shaking his head back and forth as if saying "No" while holding his log book.

These two men of the death search obligingly with protocol sign into Officer Jackson who them allows them in.

Jackson hands Dominic a copy of the present documented preliminary findings. This he prepares for the homicide detectives assuming this duty, declaring, "Here she is."

Dominic and Leo both perform a quick scan while approaching an officer taking notes talking to another.

Dominic asks, "Jefferson, what stands out on your preliminary survey,"

Jefferson replies, "Young white female. Head shots. No eye witnesses. No one heard a thing. We couldn't find spent shell casings. Nothing else found so far except weird footprints in the crust of the remaining snow and trash.

These two who follow the pathways taken by the grim reaper next make contact with the crime scene photographer Danny and his documenter, Joe, who are now taking pictures of pediatric nurse Luna peacefully laid to rest in her car.

Their main camera is set on a tripod with a large close-up lens. Over one of Danny's shoulders is a satchel containing photographic equipment. A regular camera hangs down his other shoulder.

Danny instructs Joe that, "OK, we got the body shots. Now we'll get the car's contents starting with her purse on the passenger side seat, then the back seat."

Joe, writing in his log book relates, "Well, they're here."

Without getting in Danny's way, Dominic slightly leans forward requesting, "Danny, send us copies of everything you take along with your documents."

Danny interrupted by the sound of Dominic's voice, without turning says, "If it ain't the gruesome twosome."

Dominic, "I see nepotism's still grand."

Joe, continuing the sarcasm, "In a way you gotta know, but in our case it's genetic. We're artists, and our sister is still not dating you."

Leo asks Danny, "What's your initial impression, and what do you think now?"

Danny replies, "First a usual argument killing. But this one seems different, to efficient."

Joe said that he would bring them over.

Leo authoritatively tells Danny, "I'll look over the body after you're done. The coroner's people can finish here, then take her for a better examination.

Continuing his investigation, Dominic meanders to an officer holding a flashlight looking down by a bush while another officer is kneeling studying something to the ground.

The officer holding flashlight, Lincoln, looks toward Dominic and reported, "These are weird footprints."

The kneeling officer, Washington, without taking his eyes off the footprints relates, "We're ready to take make a cast once they're photo'd."

After inspecting Luna's remains, Leo makes his way to the hospital security guard and says, "We'll need to see your surveillance tapes from before the time she left work. Officer Jackson will assign someone to accompany you."

Finally, Dominic finds Leo saying, Time to interview the maternity ward. We'll re-group early tomorrow."

"I, Satan, accuse you of choosing to strike others with sharp ends of thornbushes from the dark hardened recess in your hearts, minds, and souls.

Your habits are peculiar among all other creatures.

You self-justify falsely moralizing and defining reasons for your actions.

You turned your backs against the perfect creation of wholeness to your creation meant by the most Holy-Almighty."

OPPOSITES

"I, Satan, says humanity is born to fully experience and share life with others. Our creation was conceived and designed to be completely developed functionally gregarious creatures.

Being so is wonderous.

When two are in union they become one. Our affirmations give confirmation to the well-being for those whom we share existence. Reciprocation does the same for all.

Such is the everlasting design for us from the shared one most Holy-Almighty."

The hallowed halls of the police station in the early morning are bustling with the familiar air of low intensity angst. Dominic and Leo quietly walk through a corridor to their office.

Passing the vending machine area Dominic asks, "Want coffee?"

Leo nods 'yes.' Leaving with their bag of bagels he says, "I'll get my notes ready."

When Dominic waits for the second cup of coffee to fill, he hears something unfamiliar to these corridors. He moves to look down the hallway in the opposite direction of Leo's exit.

Through the haze of officers and staff walking in various directions, he sees a woman walking alone toward his direction.

She's dressed as a statement and obviously out of place: very prim, proper and professional with blouse underneath a jacket buttoned to her neck and with padded shoulders. With this was a thick loosely wrapped matching tie. Long sleeves are fashioned at the wrists. She is carrying an oversized briefcase with one hand. Her purse is slung over her other shoulder.

Dominic hears the tapping of her high heel shoes clicking the floor becoming louder.

As this lady is passing, she sees Dominic with a cup of coffee in one hand picking up another cup that is on the top of the vending machine.

She drops her briefcase with a thud, asking, "I know I'm close. Where's Alighieri and McFarland's area?"

Dominic points with his coffee cupped hand to an open entrance leading to a large room full of desks and people.

Dominic directs, "Take a left at the first aisle. It's in the corner. Back of the bus – so to speak. Not far."

She thanks Dominic who then says, "I'm going that way. Want a cup?"

He still does not tell her who she is.

The woman says, "Yes. Cream and sugar."

Dominic turns getting coins from his pocket.

She takes a long pause for a deep breath and picks up her briefcase.

As the woman leaves Dominic puts the money in the vending machine and makes the selection.

Waiting for the lady's coffee to disperse from the vending machine Dominic says quietly to himself, "Figures."

Dominic then takes a peek at her walking off toward their work station with a brisk short, heel clicking determined steps.

The heavy briefcase makes her shoulder droop.

The lady's ankle buckled because of her awkwardness in the burdened high heels.

And then, Dominic thinks to himself, 'This may prove to be a moment of inspiration."

Approaching Dominic and Leo's work area she takes the feminine instinctive 5 second scan to check it out.

She observed two desks placed next to the inner work station wall touching back-to-back sideways to the work area entrance.

On the back side of each desk is a small bookshelf.

Leo is sitting at his desk looking down at his notes. Behind him are photos of men in uniform.

On the other side desk is an orderly workplace with an empty chair. On the bookshelf, the books are tidy in upright position. Placed on his back wall are family photos arranged neatly.

Leo is ignoring while deep in thought. He remains intently looking down arranging his notes as if he had not heard the rhythmic sounds of her footsteps.

This morning Leo is shaved, hair combed and looking tired.

She fumbled getting her briefcase on the desk and accidentally hits some of Leo's clutter.

The clutter moves tipping over a little stand with three flags on it. Their flag holder is positioned directly in the center where the two flags are touching.

Leo grabs it with an annoyed look and turns his back to her while reverently putting the flag stand against the back where the two bookshelves are meeting.

It has three flags. To the right is Navy; at the top the American; and, to the left is the Marine Corps flag.

The woman doesn't see what Leo is doing because she is now fumbling in her purse.

She explains, "I'm Dr. Alverado the new psychologist. I've been assigned by Dr. Williams to analyze the nurse's murder."

Leo without looking up while now arranging his notes back to whatever proper order was for them. He thinks, "What in the world is this woman doing?"

He responds with a long slow low annoyed drawl, "Aaaaand?"

Leo then looks up at her. His expression changes to 'Babe in my presence' stupefaction.

Now, Leo changes his tone with a polite, "May I help you."

Dr. Alverado, as Leo was talking, doesn't see his expression. She is busy pulling out two business cards from her purse.

She says while presenting one to Leo, "The woman killed last night. Dr. Williams asked me to come here."

Angela checks Leo over a little more closely as he is looking at her card.

Leo, while looking at her business card, replies, "That just happened, why the rush? Overtime is killing everyone."

While Leo was asking Dr. Alverado, Dominic walks in with their three cups of coffee explaining, "For what it's worth, here's the coffee. Spilled a little."

He gives Dr. Alverado her cup first.

Then Dominic hands Leo his cup.

Leo cleans off a little area of his desk in the front and away from the stand holding the three flags and puts down his cup of coffee.

While Dominic is moving around to his chair looking at her card in one hand and coffee cup in the other hand, he gestures to the empty chair behind Dr. Alvarado next to another work space. While stating, "Grab the seat next to the wall."

Dominic finishes with, "It's a wonderful day in the neighborhood. Tell us why you're here Dr. Alvarado."

Dr. Alvarado responds, "Please, Angela is fine."

Dominic replies, "Fair enough. I'm Domnic. My partner is Leo."

Angels disgustingly thinks, 'Why didn't he tell me when he was getting the coffee?"

Leo remains silent.

Angela looks back and moves up the chair. She takes her briefcase off their desks putting it on the floor.

She sits with a sigh of relief holding her purse on her lap.

She answers, "I'm here because of the nurse's homicide."

Dominic asks Angela, "You're new here?"

Angela notices the change of subject, akin to his previous noncommittal.

With a straight face she observingly replies, "Yes, and I was told you two are just the guys I need to break me in."

Dominic and Leo look at one another and Leo responds, "Well, uh, OK."

Dominic looks at Angela and says, "I'm positive you're just the asset we need."

Then looking at Leo, Dominic continues with a smile, "We're a little confused."

Leo looks at Dominic and turns to Angela asking, "Tell us about you."

A short pause occurs and Dominic chuckling to himself teasingly says to Leo, "Well Leo, continue the thought."

Leo looks at Dominic with an expression of betrayal turns to Angela and not knowing anything else to say responds, "I was born in Thailand where my father was working."

Leo knows he has been caught.

Dominic then relates, "I was born in Lucca, Italy and came to the United States when I was nineteen."

Dominic and Leo now look at Angela. The game is on.

Angela in a requital manner defers by asking, "May I get comfortable? These shoes are killing me."

Leo quickly responds, "Yes."

Dominic with a hand gesture, "By all means."

Dominic and Leo still look at Angela in silence wondering how this encounter will play out.

Angela takes off her heels and rubs the ankle of the foot she tripped with.

Sharply and concisely, she fesses up, "I'm from Central California graduated from and took the opportunity to come here for graduate school. I worked on campus and around to make living expenses. Double majored, so it took me a little longer."

After a brief pause while the two sleuths are still looking at Angela, Dominic says, "And."

Angela changing feet and starting to rub her other foot, "I was very fortunate to grow up where my parents have orchards and livestock."

While Dominic and Leo are still looking at Angela, Leo making ignorance says, "Well."

Then placing both feet on the floor and wiggling her toes Angela looks up at them.

Then Angela curtly describes, "I learned a lot about human behavior by observing animals. What they do naturally and afterward."

Dominic knowing the game is over fiddles with the flag stand replacing it a just so position.

He then requests, "Let's get down to the reason you're here."

As Dominic is getting his notebook, Leo reaches for the bag of bagels on the inside corner of his desk, takes one out and flips it to Dominic.

He then looks toward Angela and asks, "Blueberry or whole wheat?"

Angela states she is not hungry and wants neither.

Leo then looks at Dominic announcing, "I'm sure the cream cheese is still good."

Leo next opens the cream cheese, spreads it on his bagel with a pocket knife and puts the cream cheese on Dominic's desk.

Angela observes Leo, then Dominic's phone rings.

Dominic answers, acknowledges what is said with a, "Yes sir."

He relates Chief Kenny wants them. Nurse Luna's boyfriend is ready to be questioned, beckoning Angela to come.

Angela puts her shoes back on, and hold on to her purse while waiting for the two men to get ready.

Dominic rises first, then all leave.

Leo walks behind them observing the scenery.

Angela breaks the silence between her and Dominic in a low sounding motherly fashion with, "You're such a prince."

Dominic, with a smile, quickly informs Angela, "Carrying your briefcase – and I know Charlene."

They negotiate the building's maze to an interrogation area where Chief Kenny is waiting.

When they arrived Chief Kenny instructs, "You two will do the interview, Dr. Alvarado and I will observe outside."

Kenny opens the door for Dominic and Leo, then goes to stand by with Angela. The transporting officer accompanies outside.

Leo stands aside. Dominic leans against the now closed door looking at the boyfriend sitting down by a desk with a box of Kleenex at the back end of the desk. A wastebasket is under the desk.

Dominic next steps forward. Using a firm tone he asks, "What were you doing last night? Understand we are recording this interview."

The young man looks up directly at Dominic with a shocked appearance. His eyes were red and he had a wet nose.

Sensing, Dominic steps back nodding to Leo.

Leo sits in the chair meant for the interviewing officer saying, "Please tell us what happened. We need your help."

Sitting across the table from the boyfriend, leaning slightly forward and looks as if he's studying the boyfriend in a concerned way.

The boyfriend is visibly upset and passively leans toward Leo with slumped shoulders.

The boyfriend says, "She phoned and told me to pick her up at home an hour later than I was supposed to. When I got home, she didn't answer and I phoned her work. They told me she left an hour ago. That's after the time when she phoned. I went back to my car, waited a few minutes then phoned her work again. They had security go out and he - - - found her."

Then the boyfriend grabs a Kleenex and wipes his upper lip.

Leo politely states, "Thank you. Here is my card if you think of something. You're free to go."

Leo gets up out of the chair.

Dominic then quietly says, "If you don't mind, we might require another interview and a polygraph later."

With his head tilted back and looking directly at Dominic, the boyfriend nods 'yes.'

Dominic now hands the boyfriend his card, "These things require all the help we can get. So, if you think of anything else, please contact either of us."

They all quietly depart the interrogation room.

After the boyfriend left, the guard said, "That was quick."

Leo replies, "He's devastated. This wasn't a gas chamber exercise."

Guard asks, "What?"

Leo replies, "It's the only time a man doesn't feel guilty when letting another man see his tears, especially with all snot running out of his nose. Men don't fake that that easily."

The guard slightly looks down nodding yes with 'I should have remembered that' look.

Kenny obligingly taps Leo's shoulder and says, "Thanks doc. Doctors Williams and Alvarado will analyze the video."

Angela excuses herself to return to her supervisor Dr. Williams lugging her briefcase with her.

Dominic surmises with Kenny that, "He'll stick around."

Kenny, "You won't need to use any antics on the kid. Back to that cave you guys have for an office and bring me an answer."

While returning to their work station Dominic chuckles to himself quietly saying, "Charlene."

Leo hears this and asks, "Charlene? What are you thinking?"

Leo then says, "Sometimes I wonder about your ancient state of mind."

Dominic paternally iterates, "Maybe you should have grabbed some of those Kleenexes to wipe of the wet behind your ears."

And Leo shoots back to Dominic a 'What the hell does he have in mind' look.

Dominic and Leo now have two cups of coffee each with the bagels and cream cheese on their desk amply dispersed.

Dominic gets to the point, "The killer's anger was focused during the assault. It does not involve sexual satisfaction."

Leo, "More often than not he experienced a childhood trauma."

Dominic says, "Let's look into the shooting. Start getting into this character's mind. More likely than not a male"

Leo, while dunking part of a bagel with cream cheese, starts, "Modus Operandi."

Dominic, "Attacked at night."

Leo, "No witnesses."

Dominic, "Planned escape route."

Leo, "Car parked in hospital parking lot. Need bus schedules."

Dominic, "Brought weapon."

Leo, "Not a weapon of opportunity."

Dominic, "No shell casings."

Leo, "At least two shots. A double tap probably. He must have kept the spent cartridges."

Dominic, "Funny footprints by bushes. How?"

Leo, "Stalked her."
Dominic, "Organized or Disorganized?"
Leo, "Organized."
Dominic, "Victimology?"
Leo, "Female."
Dominic, "Young."
Leo, "Light hair. Not totally blond.
Dominic, "Nurse."
Leo, "Pediatric."
Dominic, "Boyfriend."
Leo, "Need to check past boyfriends."
Dominic, "Possible ex-husband."
Leo, "Parents, family, friends."
Dominic, "The Signature will have to wait."
Leo, "Okay, the photos when ready."

And Sanguineri pondering his victims, thinks, 'Everywhere they sit, they spin their evil webs believing the world revolves around them.'

"I, Satan, accuse you of taking the oppositions you create in your minds to violence on the others you were meant to be with.

You think you made a bonding to your desire, yet you create disunity that lives in veiled darkness.

You humans were made to possess moments of ecstasy that should take you winging to heavenly heights.

You may be happy, but without bliss.

Your defilements create those who can but fly — yet never soar. You end up living not knowing the wonders of you both, while not knowing your loss."

POSTPARTUM

"I, Satan, remind you that a blessing given by the most Holy-Almighty is paramount.   All blessings bestowed are to be taken seriously with reverence.

Whatever the blessing, sanctity is attached.

Blessings given are the decision of the most Holy-Almighty whether asked for or not.

A blessing entails a duty.   Treat that blessing properly. They are to be nurtured and protected.

Blessings, however given, are never to be rejected."

Angela enters the Forensic Psychology department headed by Dr. Williams.

The office manager, Charlene, is standing next to her desk organizing paperwork.

Seeing Angela come in, Charlene gets right to the point, "The fly will watch the spider build her web – So?"

Angela, "My ankle still hurts from those heels. I feel like Clutzilla."

Charlene, having learned from the investigators then asks, "Well?"

Angela, "This outfit makes me look like a postage stamp."

Charlene then asks, "And?"

Angela, "They're predictable. But I'll have to figure out what is occupational and what is from them just being men."

Charlene, with a smirk says, "It depends on what your initial impression. Tell me?

Angels, "Yes."

Charlene with a smirk, "You're avoiding."

Angela, "You're beginning to sound just like them."

Charlene with an all-knowing-look states that, in their own way each will be doing a bit of training on each other.

Angela blurts out, "Are you their sister, or have you been around them too long?"

Changing the subject Angela follows with, "Is Dr. Williams available?"

Charlene pointing to Dr. Williams' office door responds, "Yes."

Before entering Dr. Williams's office, Angela looks back at Charlene and with a smirk says, "You're right."

Now in a stronger whisper, "See how I, Sanguineri, have mastered but the ways my meeting with you will be but a brief unknowing.

Something is happening this evening with utmost importance to certain people."

Outside the Boston Hilton Back Bay well dressed women come and go. Conversations of those leaving echo praises of the party they just came from.

Inside the front lobby is a sign announcing Greater Boston Area Cosmetic Convention with an arrow pointing to the location.

Through an open door in a large room can be seen different companies demonstrating their products.

It is easy to center one's eye on the closest few booths next to the wide double door open entrance.

A middle-aged woman is demonstrating at one of the booths.

Sanguineri muses, 'Everyone claims their rights, while granting those rights to others is a matter of toleration.'

This demonstrator proclaims, "We are on the cutting edge of research. Our products are developed to be the best in removing wrinkles and give you fresh newborn skin. Even Oprah endorsed this research."

The first customer, who looks similar to nurse Luna asks, "What is your active ingredient."

Demonstrator, "Most of our products have pentapeptides now. They have been proven to be extremely effective. They byproduct is in all lipsticks."

The second customer states, "What man would want to kiss that. I've heard that they are made from…"

The demonstrator interrupts in a louder than usual voice without letting the second lady finish.

Then she says to the first customer, "Oh, the industry just calls them peptides now. Here, feel how smoothly it can be applied."

A third lady snipingly states, "I don't care where it comes from. Don't tell me. All I care about is if it works for me."

The first customer smiles applying the cosmetic on her face stating, "I see it really penetrates evenly."

The demonstrator keeps her focus on the first lady as the second customer walks away.

Sanguineri departs the hotel to dine elsewhere.

Later in the evening the demonstrator leaves prepared to continue for the next day's event.

She reaches her SUV, opens the back to put in what she does not want to leave behind and closes the back hatch. She moves to her driver's door.

Her head winces. She stumbles and falls.

No gunshots were heard, only arrested puffs. Then a packet is seen thrown onto her body bouncing off.

Sanguineri instructs, 'The basic test of freedom is perhaps less in what we are free to do than in what we are free not to do.'

Driving to the crime scene Dominic says to Leo, "It's a relief you transferred to the Ready Reserves. Concentrate on their correspondence courses and studies.

Leo sadly chimes in, "Yeah, but will miss it. It's time to go."

Then on a serious note Leo says, "Too many things are dragging into each other."

On arriving they see the crime scene is similar to nurse Luna, but obviously in a different location.

Squad cars, ambulance, tow truck, taped off, and everywhere officers are busy.

Dominic reminiscently spoke lightly, "Let's see what he did."

The two investigators walk up to Officer Jackson and sign in. Jackson says, "This one is almost the same as the one last night."

Leo surmises, "Probably the same perp. Most of these guys have no burn-out point. He won't stop until something or someone stops him."

Dominic, "the seeking of one thing shall find another."

Leo, "Let's hope it is something we can use."

Leo leaves and goes to the medical examiner who has already arrived.

Dominic searches out the photographers and Joe said, "Like one shot, one kill. But, another double tap."

Danny, "Another bag. He's communicating to us."

Dominic then finds Officer Lincoln again searching with a flashlight who tells, "Same funny footprints."

Officer Washington, again with Lincoln, surmises, "It looks like something was put over his shoes."

Dominic asks, "Who's doing the Crime Kit."

Officer Madison signifies, "Davis."

Dominic walks to Officer Davis asking, "What'cha finding?"

Davis says in a Southern drawl, "Both appear locations. Evidence also includes a bag. We're about ready to cast all the footprints. Fingerprints are being processed."

Leo, with the coroner's staff, inspects the body ready for transfer, with the Fire Rescue team having the gurney there, and one holding the ready body-bag.

Leo finds Dominic reporting that, "Coroner's ready to take her."

Dominic to Leo. "Preliminary's about done."

Davis, "Jackson will get the detailed report to you once they check this scene in daylight."

Upon leaving Dominic and Leo report out to Jackson.

Dominic asks, "Is your preliminary similar?"

Jackson, "Almost to a Tee. Early evening kill. Parking Lot," and gives Leo a copy of the preliminary report.

Dominic, "Let's see what hotel security has and call it a day."

Leo unfolds the victim identification paper Jackson gave him and says to Dominic while opening his cell phone, "I'll leave a message with Dot to get victim stats started and ask Cookie if she can work a miracle. Get rolling tomorrow."

Dominic says, "Progress."

First thing in the morning, Dominic and Leo go to the Crime Lab and find Cookie.

Dominic asks, "What's the run down so far?"

Cookie walks them to a technician's desk and picks up some photos and two packets. She gives the pictures to Leo and the packets to Dominic.

Cookie, "Good fortune might be in order gentlemen. Footprint size and shape appear to match. But look at this."

Cookie takes the blunt side of a pen and pointing to a picture Leo is holding, "Notice no tread, surface irregularities and lines. Something is covering them."

Cookie takes back the photos and hands them back to the technician.

Then Cookie continues, "Kenny also wants a copy of these."

Leo says to Cookie, "One's a nurse. Check out if they can be any medical over-slippers. The thing's is hiding the shoes could be cut cardboard or over the counter inserts."

Looking at Dominic, Leo continues, "They're great for Boon-Dockers. The new ones are almost as good as tennis shoes."

Keeping the pace forward Dominic asks, "Ballistics?"

Taking them to the Ballistic Lab, cookie says, "It would be nice to have shell casings. But the electron scan shows the metallurgy of the bullet fragments match."

A technician brings out two scans. Dominic and Leo look at them quickly.

On the move toward the exit, Cookie says, "Photos you've seen are in the packets. We're still waiting for the surveillance tapes. Chief Kenny is pushing us, so be prepared.

Dominic thanks cookie then tells Leo that, "It's time to check if Dot has anything."

Dominic and Leo reach the Record's Office, and approach dot.

Leo asks, "Do you have any files ready yet."

She takes two files out of a stack saying, "They're here."

She gives one to Leo and the other to Dominic.

Dot continues, "Legal is working to get the rest. Last night's victim's Ex has already lawyered up."

Dominic thanks Dot and they leave to their lair.

Dominic walks into their work area alone. He places dot's file and Cookie's packet on the outside of his desk.

Then Dominic puts Leo's file and packet on his desk area next to a fresh bagel bag that's his turn to buy.

Dominic goes back to his side, sits, takes out his notes and nurse Luna's file from one of his desk's drawers and also places these on his desk.

Then Dominic leans back.

Shortly after Leo walks in, gives Dominic his coffee and machine pastry, places his coffee on the side of his desk and sits.

Dominic lifts up his coffee and toasts, "Here's to the computer age and its promise to decrease paperwork."

Leo toasts back with a little raising gesture of his coffee and takes a gulp.

Now they both concentrate for the moment on their coffee, bagel and pastry.

Leo says, "Break time." Takes a breath and exhales through his clenched teeth.

After a five second pause Dominic says, "Break's over. This doesn't add up. We have to run the drill to organize the clutter. Let's begin by comparing our notes and Dot's stuff of both victims at the same time.

They start their ritual of sifting through findings and paperwork.

Dominic, "OK, first things first. The two crime scenes. What's there and what's not there."

Leo, "Different types of vehicles."

Dominic, "Both shot while their vehicles are in workplace parking lot."

Leo, "Right after work in the evening."

Dominic, "Matching head wounds."

Leo, "Two each."

Dominic, "No shell casings."

Leo, "Weird footprints which he disguised."

Dominic, "No witnesses – nada for either. Still need surveillance tapes.""

Leo, "A paper bag was near each,"

Dominic, "The second killing is similarly Organized. Clearly not Disorganized."

Dominic changes focus, "OK. Victimology. Let's find similarities and dissimilarities. Obviously both victims were female."

Leo, "Again, both leaving work."

Dominic: "Last known contact?"

Leo, "First the nurse was with other nurses, nuns and security.

Dominic, "Yes physically, but later on the phone with her boyfriend."

Leo, "No known last contact yet for the second victim."

Dominic, "Different ages."

Leo, "one in her middle twenties, never married, no kids, boyfriend."

Dominic, "Other in her early forties, divorced, two kids in her custody, no known relationship."

Leo, "Different color, length and hair style,"

Dominic, "Vastly different professions, but both wearing work clothes."

Dominic continues, "Different body type, but not too dissimilar."

Leo, "Different DMV and credit ratings."

Dominic says, "The nurse's DMV is clean. Cosmetics has six parking tickets which seems kinds pretentious."

Leo, "Yeah, and her credit score is on the brink with all these cards."

Dominic, "Cosmetics got everything. How can she afford it? We gotta research their daily routines."

Leo, "Yeah, lifestyle, habits, friends."

Dominic, "Maybe there is something in her medical history. Need to contact the family."

Dominic continues, "Know you're ready for the photos to find something relevant."

Leo, "Right now my bagel is relevant. That pastry wasn't enough"

Repeating their morning ritual Leo reaches into the ever-ready bagel bag, takes one out along with the cream cheese. He spreads some cream cheese on the bagel, breaks it in two and dunks one piece in his coffee, then takes a bite and a gulp.

Dominic finishes pastry, then a drink, and looks over the pictures neatly laid out on his desk, saying, "One day you will go for a steak dinner and try to dunk your baked potato in a glass of wine. Messy and polluting."

Almost half a minute goes by in Dominic's pensive dining, while Leo thumbs through Danny and Joe's pictures like a deck of cards. Then Dominic asks, "Now what's relevant?"

Leo says, "Now back to square one. Same Organized M.O. and same ritual of a bag."

Dominic, "The contents of the ritual will give us the Signature meaning to his behavior."

Leo replies, "There's an owl in the nurse's bag."

Moving on Dominic queries, "What does a single young lady spend her money on?"

Leo now with a mouth full of crumbly with soaked babel in his mouth attempts, "What?"

Dominic, "Cosmetics and primping things." Then jokingly says, "One day you might need to know."

Leo, "I'll wait to have a wife and teen-age girls. Here we're mushrooms though he's feeding us his message."

Dominic, "OK. The cosmetics rep.'s bag had a stuffed toy animal. It's a pig with a gold ring in its nose."

Leo, "And it looks like he spent time sewing it in the way he wanted to. That little ring cost a bit. Both contents are pretty generic and might be hard to trace."

Dominic with one eyebrow raised and a deliberate deeper voice slowly says, "Patience is a virtue, it requires practice."

Dominic continues normally, "Drs. Williams and Alvarado will need time to do their analysis. We'll have to gumshoe the haystack hoping to find the needle."

In a large official looking office is a man who appears authoritative. He stands behind his large desk in front of a window looking out. There are two neatly dressed men facing him close to the shut door.

This man in charge, the Chief Agent, informs the two, "We're in a spot."

Agent 1, "To the best of our knowledge he's now been tracked through five locations in the US"

Agent 2, "He's now only one step ahead of us, but still not good. We need to know where he going to go to."

Chief Agent, "Thet means more like three steps. It's going to go public. Who knows what will happen if they put the pieces together. You've never met him."

Both Agents say, "No sir."

Chief Agent, "He most assuredly will, as they say, improvise, adapt and overcome."

Agent 1, "Then it's known why he is doing this?

Chief Agent, "The CIA has done two studies on this type of behavior but have refused to make them public. They know, but how much they know we aren't sure. Stay on him."

Agent 2: "Communications?"

Chief Agent relates, "I want daily. Updates should be faster from the field.

"I, Satan, still accuse you that you reject your blessing given designed in perfection by the most Holy-Almighty.

To the most Holy-Almighty this rejection is criminal never to be forgiven.

You humans are a violent creation given the sentient conscious to mediate your behavior. You are a consistently failing creature like none other. Your disorders tend to be cruel repetitions and violence to satisfy bloodthirst.

Your ancestors have been forever doomed. Cease or you too will meet the same fate."

INFANCY

"I, Satan, says: You are to honor and cherish that which you bring forth.

This is demanded by the most Holy-Almighty.

Your union is as a mother most holy with the father most almighty.

Deep inside through your unity, is future made.

Future in all creation belongs to who follow from you, then from them to pass likewise.

This is inheritance of existence in which both creation and that which inherits is not to be defiled."

Sanguineri's now childlike voice, "Where does the newborn go from here."

Often the human condition starts with: What the young one begs for, the grown-up throws away."

In one contemporary doctor's office, that of a pediatrician, there is another nurse who takes a young infant wrapped in a blue blanket from his mother.

She says to the mother, "You must understand it is for their own good."

Then she carries the infant to a room putting the chart inn the door's chart.

She enters the room with the baby and closes the door where the not so secret of secrets will prevail.

The pediatrician arrives, takes the chart and turns to listen to another nurse walking up.

She informs, "The parents are a little anxious."

Pediatrician, "Go ahead and strap him down. Then, I'll give him a shot."

This second nurse walks to the reception area to reassure the parents again.

The doctor opens the chart, looks, then walks over and shuts the door.

The nurse returns to the business office saying to the receptionist, "Guess if a woman is given the date rape drug so she won't feel or remember it, a rape did not occur."

Receptionist, "So much for equal rights and protection."

The nurse looks at the treatment room soulfully saying, "She's starting too soon. We all can hear it."

Receptionist replies, "Such a deal."

Nurse, "Some have said infants don't feel pain."

Receptionist, "In their hearts everyone knows different, whether they admit it or not."

Nurse, "Soon I'll have to go in and monitor his vitals until the initial acute shock is over and he is ready to be given back to his parents."

Receptionist laments, "The ACLU and Amnesty International refuse to exist for them legally."

For at this moment in the infant's inward moving mind reality is blanked, and it is as if fireworks are exploding inside from excruciation.

Sanguineri reminds, "Parenting has individual significance and social consequences."

This day is leisurely spent by Sanguineri preparing for events yet to come. His gear had come previously. All appears in shipshape condition.

After stowing his gear, he enjoyed a relaxing lunch before his reconnaissance. And finally, he thinks, 'Everyone is the offspring of their actions.'

It is early evening with darkness mounting. Sanguineri parks at the Boston Medical Center and plants tracking devices underneath intended vehicles.

He walks the pavement outlining winter's sleeping ground while passing the cars parked.

A special mental note is of the location of the Obstetrics and Gynecology Department.

Keeping an ever-moving slow pace of an old man, he kept an eye on the entrance as employees left work.

A woman walked out carrying a briefcase and has a stethoscope around her neck. He keeps distance on the sidewalk studying where she is going.

Her gait is fast. Having closed the distance, she gets into her car, leisurely fixes her hair, backs out and drives off.

Retribution knows people are creatures of habit. This day of the week should be no different. He gets into his car, picks up a tracking device and turns it on.

He takes of assured of his pursuit.

Sanguineri closes the distance as she drives into the parking lot of the Faneuil Mall Market Place.

He is confident she will continue her usual pattern centering on the Quincy Market. Then she will pick a place to dine.

Afterward she will walk the mall with its little shops stopping here and there at the most interesting places of this evening's whim. He thinks, 'Bad habits are as infectious by example, as a plague by contact.'

The evening is less than an hour older as Sanguineri pulls back into the Boston Medical Center's parking lot. It is now dark. The time to prowl.

Another woman's figure walks into the parking lot, also gets into her car, backs out and leaves.

Sanguineri, turning on another tracking device, follows for a short time to the outskirts of the town and into a residential street.

While driving he thinks, 'Right cannot rest on madness.'

They are now almost alone, two cars with juxtaposed life forces. The cardiologist stops at a light in the left-hand lane going straight.

Sanguineri drives up in the left-hand turn lane next to her with car windows down. Then he leans over to the passenger side and drops out a bag.

There is a pause before the touching.

When the few cars in cross traffic goes through the intersection, the light for its traffic turns yellow.

The light turns green for them and they both get ready then start to proceed.

He turns left, and her car rolls forward crossing the intersection, veering a little right until it jumps the curb and rests. Then, there is the fate of oblivion.

Driving away Sanguineri with a stronger childlike voice says aloud, "Our technology has exceeded it humanity."

Keeping on his prepared schedule, Sanguineri returns back to the Faneuil Mall Market Place.

He waits until his next purification returns to her car. She puts her shopping bags of instant treasures in her trunk and departs.

Sanguineri follows her with its tracking device to an apartment building where she parks.

He parks on the other side of the road allowing time for her to collect her belongings.

The Obstetric and Gynecologist physician walks to her outside lower-level flat's entrance where the porch is lighted with shrubs waist high in front of the road.

Three quick skillful puffs are heard. Two find their mark, the other the outside wall. She drops.

Sanguineri drives off and tosses his trademark paper bag onto the street. It lands close to the gutter.

He muses, 'No one was ever endowed with a right without being at the same time saddled with a responsibility.

By now the cardiologist's first crime scene was well organized with all the elements present: tow truck, ambulance, coroner's car, three police sedans, photography vehicle and Leo with Dominic.

Officer Lincoln first found the bag containing its object lesson in the middle of the street outside the taped off section of the curb across the street.

The coroner's staff member inspects the body thinking, "This is too similar for comfort."

Lincoln informs Danny of the bag to be photo'd while Jackson gives Dominic a copy of his preliminary notes.

Jackson says, "Something more is going on. We've just been assigned as a special Crime Scene Unit for shootings not gang or drug related and fits this M.O."

Leo says to Dominic and Jackson, "She's been double-tapped."

Jackson, "That's what I mean. The guy's too good not to be trained."

Dominic, "Let's coordinate communications. Each team will be assigned the same vehicle and a list of who's assigned will be made for each one. Preliminary rolls should be determined. We need everyone's cell phone number."

Timing has a lot to do with success. It is pitch dark outside now. Sanguineri's car drives into an open parking space outside Pediatrician's home.

He turns off the third tracker. For now, he settles in to observe behind heavily tinted windows. He has the time to enjoy his super-sized fast food. He has two large coffees in the cup holders and a couple of canned sodas.

Eventually the pediatrician's figure appears in front of a window through lace curtains. It is the right window this time.

All that can be heard, as usual, are the suppressed sounds from an automatic weapon set to three-burst.

The window shatters, the figure drops from sight.

Sanguineri places the automatic weapon with noise suppressor on the passenger floor and drives away.

He throws the bag toward her condo reflecting, 'If you create an act, you create a habit. If you create a habit, you create a character. And, if you create a character. You create a destiny.

And all the events are duly recorded.

Meanwhile back at the cardiologist's crime scene the tow truck with the dead doctor's car and the ambulance with the body are gone. So too the coroner.

Patrol cars are still present with their lights flashing. As well as the photographers. And crime scene collectors are coming the area observing, finding, and taking notes.

Dominic and Jackson are standing together. Leo is with the rest exchanging information.

Lincoln briskly comes to Dominic and Jackson with the news. We've got another one. I told Dispatch to have the responding unit to look for a bag." As he gives Jackson a piece of paper.

Then Jackson gives Dominic papers for his report and the location of the new crime scene given by Lincoln.

Jackson called a group meeting in the field.

Jackson says, Listen up. Another team is coming to secure a watch here until morning. We're going to a new killing. Come and write down the address.

Dominic motions to Leo to come over and says to Jackson, "Meet you there."

Jackson and his Crime Unit arrive as quickly as they could to take over the second crime scene.

Danny and Joe were next to the Ob-Gyn's fateful happening when Dominic and Leo arrive. The rest of the grim reaper elements came in due time.

Also present for this time's purity ritual were the press and bystanders.

Jackson approaches the duo before they get out and informs Dominic, who is always driving, "You've got company."

Leo spots, "She's here."

Angela is standing just inside the taped off crime scene with her left hand holding her right elbow and right hand raised up to her chin. She is dress street-wise.

Dominic, "Freud couched in the trenches. This is new for us."

Jackson, "I widened the crime scene to keep bystanders and the reporters at a distance. We don't know this."

Jackson registers the duo then lets them in.

Dominic asks Jackson, "Witnesses."

Jackson answers, "None."

They go to Angela, and Dominic says politely, "Nice to have the Ivory tower step over the tracks."

Angela, "Thanks."

Looking at Leo, instinctively doing a quick twist of her hair with an index finger, while saying, "Hi."

Leo looks down taking a quick peek at what she's wearing and saying, "How do?"

Dominic goes to Danny and Joe. Leo and Angela follow.

Danny muses, "There is no winning in this, only loosing."

Leo asks Joe, "Did you do a bag?"

Joe answers with, "I got it."

At the crime scene's perimeter, the tow truck operator walks up to Jackson and says, "I found another. Have a look."

Jackson and the rest look at the undercarriage and see the tracking device.

Leo says to Danny, "We can trace these."

Danny gets under the car to photograph with Joe kneeling down recording.

Jackson returns to his position.

Angela relates, Dr. Williams has asked me to accompany you from now on. Kenny agrees."

The bystanders and the press are milling about not so smartly having got close to the perimeter tape.

Leo states, "There are more of them now. They can become a pain if there are too many."

Angela responds, "The dinner bell."

Leo questions, "What?"

Angela explains, "In hunting, when people hunt deer and a bear hears a shot, the bear comes knowing there'll be a gut pile to feed on. We're here too."

The three move to the body behind the waist high bushes hiding her body from the roadside view. Reaching the body with Leo in the lead, Leo leans over.

The coroner's field agent letting Leo examine the body states, "Got the body temperature. Two wounds, one in the chest and the other in the head. They found a third in the wall."

Leo, low over the body says to Dominic who is showing Angela a marked area where the bullet has hit the entryway realizes, "He's more than trained."

Leo turns to the field agent, "Thanks, I'm done."

Then to Angela, Leo says in dark gallows humor, "Shopped 'til dropped."

Lincoln appears saying, "Third time tonight, here's the address."

Dominic and Leo drive to the site of the third cleansing, the pediatrician.

Jackson's team, having turned over the Ob-Gyn's crime scene to an evening watch, is behind them.

Bystanders are gathered outside the perimeter and the press is setting up equipment. The word is out.

They meet the officer initially overseeing the crime scene.

The Officer in Charge says, "We got the word about Jackson's team. Documentation has been started for hm and his crew. Something big must be happening for this type of coordination."

They start toward the apartment. Contract doctors and nurses move around.

Dominic, "Look at the window."

Leo looks then turns to the officer, "Witnesses?"

Officer, "Yes, they're here."

Dominic and Leo enter the pediatrician's apartment. Two policemen are waiting.

Leo goes directly to the body, looks down and then out the window.

He lines up the blown-out window to the body and sees the other side of the street taped off.

Then Leo turns to look at the inside wall where the two officers are showing Dominic bullet holes.

Dominic holds out his notebook, looks at Leo gesturing, "I'd like to see the witnesses,"

A young male with his wife, tells Dominic, always writing in his notebook, "All we heard was the window shattering."

Then, an older woman with her even older husband said to Leo, "We saw a car drive off."

Leo, "Can you describe it?"

The old husband said, "It was dark, but I could tell it was a dour door sedan and not a sports car."

Jackson arrives, and Dominic says to the two couples, "Thanks, we'll contact you later."

Dominic and Leo start walking to Jackson.

Leo surmises, "A four door sedan. Maybe our perp is older."

When they reach Jackson, Jackson is telling a patrolman and Lincoln, "Have the bag photographed first."

Dominic, Leo, Angela and Jackson all walk back toward the apartment as Danny and Joe drive up.

Angels, "I think his motive is probably cognitive revenge."

Dominic, "Revenge is often true for serial predators, but their motives can be deeply suppressed."

Angela responds, "With these killings he knows exactly why – cognitive."

Leo, "Most have had poor mother relationships. Are you talking child abuse?"

Angela, "In a way quite possibly 'yes.' From his point of view, he thinks so. The rule is that child abuse victims don't talk about it. They take up the guilt of what happened. This one will if given the chance. It will be like a Mission Statement to the world."

As they are leaving, Dominic says to Jackson, "Hopefully we get useful physical evidence and ballistics will tell us what he's using now."

As they are walking to the car, Angela suggests, "You should check these doctor's histories. Professional memberships often tell where they've practiced."

Leo now looks very seriously at Dominic saying, "This might mean the first two might be secondary like branches of a tree."

Angela, "State Boards of Medical Examiners will have records of complaints filed against the physicians. They often move after a sticky malpractice suit makes the news."

Continuing to the car, Leo says, "The whole thing is moving, but in which direction."

Dominic turns to Angela as she gets into their car, "Nurses, doctors, mothers, cosmetics, all women. What kind of web is he weaving here. What web was put in his head?"

Angela, "The more we understand him the more we stack the odds in our favor."

Leo, "Put it together and we will find the motive. Tomorrow is another day."

Dominic, "The more uncivilized a man, the surer he is that he knows what's right and what's wrong."

"I, Satan, accuse you of not cherishing that which the most Holy-Almighty has blessed you with.

You do not cherish the most Holy-Almighty that has once made you a blessing made in perfection.

The evil you have created is like a sensory deprived child who develops rhythmic movements as if banging his head against his crib so that you transfer your motions into useless prayer.

Your show of prayer is a sham to the most Holy-Almighty. Blasphemies from beginning to end."

CHILDHOOD

Sanguineri says "Unto you: Keep in your heart that life is the most precious gift you will ever receive."

Life is given freely to each and every one of you through forces above and beyond out comprehension.

Your life is to be lived fully in peace and harmony with others everywhere.

The tenet of all that is good, spoken by the good from all four corners of the world, is to treat others as you yourself should want to be treated.

This treatment is through sanity, not through perversion or aberration.

Charity is a gift freely given to those who are in need. Charity is aiding life as intended. Repent or die."

Dominic arrived early for work. On his desk was a note from Chief Kenny who wanted a briefing.

At Kenny's office drinking their coffee, Dominic was summarizing the previous evening.

Leo arrived about fifteen minutes later with bagels, pastries and doughnuts."

Leo greets, "Morning Chief."

Kenny looks at Leo asking, "Where's the jelly filled? Prefer not to eat those whole wheat bagels you eat trying to be half-way healthy. And I want nothing with poppy seeds. Golden Flow is coming"

Leo jokes back, "Chief, are you worried about your mellow attitude, or the Golden Flow? Surprise urinalysis coming up? We'll pass on the rumor."

Kenny nods to Leo and continues, "Dominic's given the rundown about last night. Do you have any leads on the shooter?"

Dominic, "Nothing yet sir."

Kenny pulls out a medium sized notebook and grabbing a pen saying, "Let me just make an entry here in my 'I Don't Give a Damn Notebook."

He rips out a page, crumples it and throws it between Dominic and Leo saying, "The Commissioner called telling me the last one was the mayor's chief concern and only talked about solving it without mentioning any of the others."

Leo responds, "Cherchez la femme."

Dominic quips, "The meaning of life. Makes the world go around – doesn't it?"

Kenny, "The way the mayor came at him, the Commissioner figures she must have been his private squeeze."

Dominic responds, "Rats scurry and the Charmin piles up higher and deeper."

Kenny with sarcasm and a twist of his head, "At critical times the authorities claim no responsibility."

Dominic, "We've got an experienced shooter."

Kenny, "You are the lead for all these killings as if there is one serial perp."

Leo, "I sense he is in a spree mode."

Dominic, "Violent offenders usually begin where they most feel comfortable. This guy must have started elsewhere a long time ago."

Leo, "They seem to find a way that works and stick to it."

Chief Kenny then informs Dominic and Leo that Dr. Ozawa is expecting them and cautions, "Be discreet about the mayor and Commissioner. For now, we're having Dr. William give assistance on a full-time basis."

Leo, "Assistance?"

Dominic, "We've met the assistance. Thought you knew."

Kenny rises from his chair approaching the two, "Get prepared Boy Scouts. Or better yet, callous up like an old salt-dog."

Leo and Dominic get up, and while leaving Dominic said to Leo, "Now as good time as any doc. I'll let Dr. Ozawa know we are coming."

Leo replied, "Been a while since I've been with him.

Mentally preparing for their visit to the coroner to better understand the artwork of this grim reaper.

They remain silent while driving to the Coroner's Office. Moments to mull over things in their heads.

Dominic, "These apartments and the drive-by are different M.Os. He's getting a lot more confident, or else he's done this a lot more times before.

Leo, "He must have escape plans. This means he has studied each killing long before hand. Three in one night tells us how highly Organized he is.

Dominic, "This guy is not *die caid au* crazy. Experienced. I keep wondering what his training was."

Leo, "Usually hate hurts the hater more than the hated. But this guy knows how to spread out the hurt.

Dominic, "So, what's the reason for his hatred?"

Leo nods silently agreeing the question.

Dominic and Leo drive into the coroner's office parking lot, find a space, and get out.

Both maintain the silence and walk toward the entrance with heads slightly bowed.

They make their way through the small somber maze to Dr. Ozawa's secretary, Ruth, where Dominic lets her know that they arrived.

Kim finds Dr. Ozawa and tells them they he is ready to see them.

The coroner is waiting as they walk in taking their respective seats.

Dominic breaks the ice, "What do you have?"

Dr. Ozawa replies, "You need other clues beyond these bodies."

Dominic asks, "Such as."

Dr. Ozawa, "When all else fails, look into psychiatric territory. That has been assigned."

Leo asks Dr. Ozawa, "May I see the bodies now? Would like to review, and see if there might be something other that might fit combat training."

Dr. Ozawa nods saying, "They're waiting for you Doc. Review the first two victims. Then we'll go over the others. They're fresh. We'll follow in a bit."

Leo, "I'm pretty sure we'll see the same. It's just I would like to get into his head."

Leo takes off his coat and fold it before placing it on his seat and walks out.

Dominic, "Go for it. Though we've been in the hurt, Dr. Ozawa and I have not been assigned to them."

After Leo leaves Dr. Ozawa knows, "He still maintains his type of respect in these matters. He needs alone time with this one. Like most people he desires the possessing the ultimate power of a healing touch."

Ozawa then asks, "How's he doing with his correspondence courses? That's the way to go for getting a good year and the 20 years for retirement.

Dominic, "He's pushing it hard to get them out of the way. He's absolutely ready to retire when this happens."

Dr. Ozawa, "As old timers say, 'I wish I stayed in.' He will retire young."

Dominic, "It never leaves."

Dr. Ozawa, "My temper wasn't meant to stay. Situations differ. There's no draft today. When I graduated, my draft age went from 26 to 35."

Dr, Ozawa and Dominic, in some contextual pose, bow a bit forward and hold their coffee cups with both hands as if warming them in the cold while staring at something not there.

Leo slowly strolls with determination down the corridors rolling up his sleeves. Leo is running the song *Is That All There Is* through his mind.

Reaching his destination two attendants are waiting by the door for him.

Inside the chilly room housing the recently deceased, the attendants give Leo a pair of gloves. Luna and the cosmetics rep are patiently waiting for Leo's examination.

While Leo is putting his on his gloves, the attendants go to Luna's body and uncover it.

75

Approaching Nurse Luna from behind her head, Leo stands and quickly scans the remains from the top of the head downward.

Leaning over, Leo first observes her matted hair from his right to his left.

Moving to her left Leo gently moves the hair away from the wound entrance, leans closer, and puts his finger in the hole while stabilizing her head.

He next repeats the procedure on the right side but with two fingers go in the exit wound.

After this he observes her forehead, eyebrows, eyes, nose, both cheeks mouth and chin.

Repositioning his leaning stance, Leo looks at her neck and both shoulders. He follows the arm closest to him to her hand which is manicured with fingernail polish. From here he moves around to the other arm and repeats the procedure.

Observing the front torso down to her pubic region Leo completes the process down both her legs to her red toenails and the tag on one of her big toes.

Leo now waves to the attendants who approach from his opposite side of Luna's body and rolls her over to expose her back. There is a red from the settled blood.

From the angle on the attendant's side Leo observes her back from toes returning up to the back side of her head.

Dominic and Dr. Ozawa have quietly entered.

Leo repeats with the cosmetics representative.

He is astonished how similar the victims had been shot. No bruises or lacerations are on either.

He also considers their few dissimilarities.

He's ready to leave.

After leaving to return to Dr. Ozawa's office, Leo straightens up.

Only now out of the room with his mouth shut can he roll his tongue over his front teeth, and look out into the void as he meanders back.

When they return, Dr. Ozawa says to Dominic, "We'll be back in a few minutes."

Dr. Ozawa leaves with Leo while Dominic pours another cup of coffee.

Dominic has not reason toto follow and see more than he did the past evening. In country 'Done That' Devil Doc Leo knows and will tell what is needed.

Dr. Ozawa with Leo watching examines and explains the three new victim's wounds.

Dr. Ozawa previously ordered x-rays. They discuss the few bullet fragments still in the body from hitting bone.

When they return, Dominic asks both, "And?"

Dr. Ozawa, "On first glance the wounds are extremely similar. No marks elsewhere. Someone might be on a rampage. Here are the first two reports. I'll send the others ASAP. Toxicology will follow."

Leo says, "This is way out of hand. I'm positive he's trained and very good at it. He has bush sense. He may also be getting help from however many directions."

Leaving to report back to Kenny, they say good-by to Ruth.

Sanguineri is now being driven to Boston's airport figuring, 'It's time for a break today.' And yet, 'They are not going to have it their way.'

77

They park in short-term parking and take a shuttle to the terminal. After baggage check and security measures Sanguineri boards a plane to Florida.

Florida is a nice place to visit, a respite from the New England winter that is soon to intensify.

When he arrives the familiar taller, thinner, balding man is waiting.

Here they personally greet and leave together.

As they are walking out the man says to Sanguineri, "We are waiting for your Boston After Action Report."

Sanguineri queries, "are preparations being completed?"

The man assures Sanguineri all is functioning well and then Sanguineri futures, "More places meet. More people to greet."

Driving back, Dominic and Leo are more relaxed. They are relieved to be back in the vehicle and entering the world of the living.

Life is for most today just another continuance without happenstance.

Leo breaks the ice this time with. "Assistance – sounds like we're going to be setting up a larger task force. Compartmentalized."

Leo then asks, "Do you think we'll become the bottom of the downhill flow?"

Dominic, "I'd like to avoid us becoming Laurel and Hardy with everyone else like the Keystone cops."

Leo, "Now you're talking in reddles. Avoid What?

Dominic laughs, "Charlene.

Leo in bewilderment, "Charlene? Why?

Dominic mockingly says, "Charlene is more relevant that you think."

Finally, Leo understands Dominic's point about Laurel and Hardy and jokes, "I see, like Ren and Stempy with Fat Albert's gang."

Dominic, "The generation gap has just been penetrated."

The first order of business when they returned was to meet Chief Kenny.

Kenny told them, "I've received a response to our feelers. He's been to St. Louis before coming here."

Surprised, Dominic responds, "That was quick. Almost too quick."

Leo states, "I don't want to let this go, but the FBI must be notified."

Kenny, "They just notified me. It might get deeper than that. But not sure how extensive this is going to get."

Dominic, "Kirwin at their office here?"

Kenny, "No. He's gone. Alcoholism got him. Don't worry, Adam's had a heart attack."

Dominic, "Who then, Weber?"

Kenny, "He's moved on. Good thing. Played the game dirty. Such a bureaucratic whiner. He could never admit a game was played on him when he found out and never corrected his deals. We'll see what happens later. Makes one think some organizations need a total reconstruction."

Dominic, "We better get back and make our reports."

Kenny, "Both of you make them perfect ship-shape condition. I'll make the necessary copies and send them out. One will go to Dr. Williams. Others include the mayor and the Commissioner."

Both detectives give an odd look at their Chief.

Kenny answers, "I said it might get more involved. Not sure yet but I smell it and want to be prepared,"

Leo nods in agreement.

The two leave for their work area.

Joe, the photographer's assistant comes to their work area with large thick manila envelopes.

Joe states, "Danny wanted you to have these ASAP. The techs really hustled. They're the three crime scene photographs from last night."

Leo, "Death is always new somewhere, meeting us, but the taste of the smell never leaves the senses."

Joe, "At least it bothers normal people trying to maintain sanity. The abnormal relish it, and can become very resourceful in making it a game. If not, then it doesn't matter if you're normally abnormal or abnormally normal." And leaves.

Leo, "It's like some kind of humanity's favorite sporting event. They fantasy is everywhere."

Dominic, "OK, we know the scenes. Let's see if we can find the Signature in the paper bags from these pictures. I'll check the cardiologist."

Leo, "The OB's had a sting ray. The barb is painted red."

Domini, "The cardiologist is a hippopotamus."

Leo, "The pediatrician's an alligator,"

Dominic, "And the nurse had an owl, while the cosmetics rep had a pig with a gold ring in its snout.

Leo, "There's no sexual assault with all of the victims. The shootings, time and conditions are part of the MO. It can change according to situation as well as refining his handiwork."

Dominic, "All the victims are women. His attacks are at a distance. They are not face to face confrontational. This means the victims are not one on one personal with the perp. It might be Mission Oriented."

Leo, "The ritual of the paper bags shouts Signature. He's sending us a message. It is the psychological factor that drives him. Sex is still a factor."

Dominic, "Sex has many demons. Sex deals with superstition, tribal lore and socially induced fear. The list is continuous. There is a connection to sex somewhere."

Leo: "OK. The crime's Signature emotionally fulfills the perpetrator, like torture is almost always a Signature."

Dominic, "No torture, for now it's only known to the perp, his personal-cause."

Leo, "Sex. Boyfriend or ex-husband is the logical start."

Dominic, "This is too varied. Practice proves more than theory, so we're back to these bag contents. Let's see if he is into some cult."

Leo, "Dominic, you are beginning to sound spooky. Next, you'll be talking about the Italian woman's evil eye thing you joke about."

Outside an official looking office area on a path under trees, the Chief Agent is walking with the same two Agents he met with before in his office.

He says, "He's in Boston. Orders for now are to prepare profile packets about every hospital director, medical and nursing society. This will go bigger."

Agent 1, "Sir, he'll be gone by then and we might be out of the shadow."

Chief Agent, "It's the only option at this time for our end. Be discreet. Contact no other agency and report only to me. We don't want this to go public."

Agent 1, "Will our superiors want anyone in the know?"

Chief Agent, "I'm positive all related agencies will find out when the time is necessary. As for the public, we just might have more like him."

Agent 2, "Does he know there will be a time for him to end it?"

Chief Agent, "Of course. But security plans regarding him have not been completely determined."

"I, Satan, accuse you of aiding, abetting and participating in perversion against the gift of life given, in all particulate matter, by the most Holy-Almighty."

These acts are aberrations enacted only by you odd human creatures.

All your enactments come with an unwarranted price in which you perform through force.

Your acts do not bring peace and harmony, but violent systems in the illusion of controlling violence.

Your charity is a sham.

Those who come from you do not deserve you."

ADOLESCENCE

Sanguineri with a stronger voice, "Be truthful instructing others, expect this when being instructed,"

This is also a tenet when entering into social contracts."

To do otherwise is deception to be returned.

Honesty and truthfulness are imperatives that cannot be separated from having respect toward others."

Relationships to be made, continued and kept a lifetime require decency.

This also applies to those under your care.

Their lives depend on it. Later yours."

Curiosity, one of Angela's best attributes buried inside her nature, has grown and taken root. For some reason this root has quickly burrowed far and wide.

The reason for its existence must be found if it is to be deemed worthy. If found worthy, it must be nourished with understanding.

Therefore, the first step requires a little research.

Initially Angela's quest turns on her computer.

Initially Angela's quest turns on her computer.

Her obvious topic is Navy Corpsmen.

She also learned the term Devil Doc who are attached with the Devil Dogs who are the Marines. And that the Marine Corps is a Corps of the Navy.

To her surprise there are many pages are available about them.

To her surprise she found out the Marine Corps was started in a colonial bar.

After browsing, she decides to check Wikipedia.

Then with that knowledge she checks out the internet about movies and documentaries.

Nothing really intrigues her but her quest is in the forefront.

But there are some specific documentaries which included Navy Corpsmen who received the Medal of Honor.

The reason for that silly little flag stand. She then in a fleeting wonder though: but how does the older one fit in thigh it also.

She discovered within the side-bars of her search that there are men who are oddly big fans of the two movies. One she could understand while the other she did not realize.

The two films are: First the one she could see men liking – *The Army of Darkness*. Afterall there are so many x-military in law enforcement. And second, the one she did not realize, is *Meet Joe Black*.

Yet more to her liking, and discovering certain things she did order some documentaries about a man named Joseph Campbell.

This guy had a lot on a cross-search. Besides a few documentaries he had a lot of books. The documentaries are: *The Power of Myth, Joseph Campbell with Bill Moyers* and *Joseph Campbell, The Hero's Journey*.

So, she made a list to remind her of some of the videos to watch, though she wasn't personally too enthusiastic about most of them.

Enough of the military and myth stuff there are some things of more prime importance a-foot for ladies – shopping.

She freshens up and tries on some outfits deciding what she wants to wear while shopping.

Angela, checking herself in the mirror once, twice, three times altogether from different positions finally makes sure her trusty credit cards are first in line for easy access.

Her adventure into the world of commerce was to buy a new pair of shoes where the heels will be shorter, thicker, and blunt, so they will be less of a problem to work in the field with the detectives walking and carry around heavy work material. This will help save her ankles.

After buying a functional pair of shoes, Angela browses the mall mindless, while thinking about her planned week-end.

Angela's final step was to pick up some of her favorite munchies and different things to drink in preparation for a long week-end ahead.

It's better than having nothing else to do and she is totally prepared to lock down and check things out. From her list she makes her first selection.

Angela has a large bowl of half-eaten popcorn. After filling her soft drink, she picks up her phone, dials, turns on the speaker and pauses the movie she is watching: *Meet Joe Black*.

Right after filling her soft drink the ringing ends and an answering voice asks, "Well."

Angela says with enthusiasm, "Charlene, you're right. This military stuff gives insights on all these guys working in the police department."

Charlene, "Well, we women have our sisterhood. And, they have their brotherhood. We know what our shared sisterhood is and we should know what the brotherhood shares."

Angela, "Would seem to make things easier to figure out what to do."

Charlene, "The stuff you're looking at shows their share male experiences, but not what they want or need when they come home."

Angela, "What are you getting at?"

Charlene, "You're the one with all those degrees. And, they don't teach most of what's needed."

Angela, "Death circles all over *Meet Joe Black*."

Charlene, "Men want a woman who will give them peace and a little comfort when they come home. It is not good to confront them with all the emotional stuff the way we women experience life."

Angela, "Come on, it can't be as simple as that."

Charlene, "True, but he won't be susceptible to your emotional needs without a little wind-down first."

Angela, "Well, that's all well and good…" then Charlene interrupts.

Charlene, "We women are at our highest value when we are young. From there it is downhill and that has to be accepted. We have a body-clock men do not have. After thirty it begins to get difficult. Men's value increases with age and need it to establish themselves."

Angela laughs, "The hard reality."

Charlene, "All senses of betrayal are killers to relationships."

Angela, "Probably the same with serial killers."

The chit-chat continued until they're finally ready to say their good-bye's and hang up.

Following an unsuccessful weekend Dominic and Leo start Monday in typical fashion.

Dominic's turn at the not-so-secret mystery breakfast is a variety of doughnuts.

After they had arranged their notes to compare and begin their fine dining the phone rings. Dominic picks it up.

Chief Kenny announces, "We're going to meet with Dr. Williams as soon as you two get there."

When they arrive at Dr. William's office Charlene possessing a quirky smile greets, "Hello gentlemen."

The crew is waiting.

Dr. Williams directing the meeting starts, "Let's brainstorm this killer from both the criminal and psychological perspectives."

Dr. Williams continues, "The perpetrator shouts that he is a male. All victims are female. Most serial killing is stranger based and typically regional. Transient serial killing is rarer and international even more rare."

Chief Kenny reports, "We sent out feelers to the FBI and police departments in cities with a population of over a million. This guy's MO matches homicides in at least three other cities: Seattle, St. Louis, and San Francisco."

Dominic adds, "He's getting more comfortable and branching out. He's perfecting his technique. Yet we feel he's had training. The MO is very organized. No fingerprints have been found and he hides the soles of his shoes with something put on over them."

Leo figures, "No fiber evidence. Also, no fiber evidence has been found. The bags are clean. No DNA. We need to think about his financing."

Angela apprises, "He sees their humanity, just wants them dead. There have been no mutilations. It's not lust."

Dr. Williams, "When bodies are assaulted and parts excised, the killer is signifying his wish to remove any vestige of humanity from the victim. Dismemberment is a sign of a Lust Murder,"

Angela, "Those who take a piece of the body owns it for whatever psychological domination they desire."

Kenny, "It is as if the world is his oyster, and he's taking his pearls of discontent."

Dr. Williams, "Once they kill mentally, the physical part will be easier. Difficulty is learning how to turn it off.:

Angella, "Force sits on reason's back. Violence breeds violence, and that, in turn, breeds insensitivity. He probably has a regressed personality and his killings are Anger Retaliatory, whatever that retaliation is."

Dominic, "Something set off his anger and resentment. His killings express controlled rage.

Angela, "He's sending a message, but has not death wish. Maybe he considers himself already dead in a way."

Angela, "A killer rarely directs his anger on the focus of his resentment. The bags indicate otherwise."

Dominic responds, "His private fantasy."

Dr. Williams, "These fantasies are cemented by age sixteen. Most of these guys have had some trauma during childhood."

Angela, "When the parents forget he is someone today, they always deny what he becomes tomorrow."

Leo, "The killings are sexual though they're not overtly sexual. If so, is the hunter hunting hunters?"

Kenny asks, "Something from his childhood?"

Angela, "Yes, from his frame of mind."

Dr. Williams expands, "Sexual sadists usually torture their victims when they are alive. No torture has occurred that we know of with his victims. His torture?"

Angela, "Signature is a personality trait. The bags ore is message – a link."

Dominic, "They contain animals. That means we need to find significant connections with them."

Angela, "The best lead now is the pig with the gold ring. It's a bible Proverb. My farmer grandmother used to tell it to us girls when we became older. Says how a woman should not act."

Dr. Williams adds, "A Mission Oriented serial killer often justifies with a religious bent."

Angela, "His decision to do this came with the force of a revelation. Like a 'Ah-Ha' went through his mind like a flash of lightening. Sometimes with a chill in the spine and a dark veil covers his insides."

Dominic, "OK. I see how the cosmetics lady relates to the pig with the ring in its nose, but all the other victims were in the health care professions."

Chief Kenny answers Dominic's chain of thought informing, "None of the others from out of town were in the health field. They appear to have been in nature movements. A type of moon worship maybe. Their bags contained different images of the moon. One was crescent. Another was a full moon. And an odd one with a full moon painted dark reddish brown."

Dr. Williams concludes, "This involves myth, paganism, and the bible. The animals represent totems. I will help you if you find a bible and Concordance to that bible. I want to keep mine here."

Leo, "Concordance?"

Dr. Williams, "It's a huge book that lists every word in the bible and where that word can be found."

Chief Kenny concludes, "Thank you doctors. We'll get on it. Finance will love this requisition."

On their way out of Dr. Williams's office, Kenny nudges Leo joking, "Don't raid a motel for a bible. I'll get them at a bookstore or on-line. Finance will just love this requisition."

The months had come and the months have passed with not more Boston homicides attributable to to the unknown subject we know as Sanguineri.

The coming spring and summer's reach of Saanguineri stretches throughout the Southeastern portion of the United States.

The specifics deemed appropriate by Sanguineri's mission permeates physicians and others in health located in Winter Haven and Miami Florida, Baton Rouge Louisiana, and Brockton near Norfolk Virginia.

Apt tokens are presented as a momentary tombstone to their misbegotten ways.

All is noted in the recorder's Book of Death.

The sleuths with their partner psychologist started their unique research into these killings but, as always, new emergencies always come to the forefront.

Now they are every so often the ones giving details to other law enforcement agencies about new killings elsewhere and adding them to their study.

Always passing on information wondering.

The FBI had taken over and now doesn't visit.

Sanguineri is looking forward to his October moment in Sacramento. Florida is nice, but over time he has grown to find humidity unfavorable.

He feels the reason habitation is possible in the American South as well as other tropical regions is air conditioning.

During his flights he stays awake so not to be out of sync with Sacramento's three-hour time difference. So, he spends just a little time reading brochures and looking down on the moving countryside below,

For the most part, he focuses on the next prize by going over past safaris and applying lessons learned and the lessons he taught himself.

Sanguineri never travels with a packet. Another will be prepared and waiting for him when he arrives at his destination.

But, with such a busy schedule he has to make a detour through Indianapolis.

An appalling event had been noticed by those in charge of Sanguineri movements.

The specific shepherdess's location of the happening made it all the worse.

This missions meeting was quick, simple and, except for the one Sanguineri touched, uneventful.

Anyway, it's onto Sacramento view the earth's surface below.

Circular irrigation patterns of Midwestern and Western desert intrigue him.

While disembarking Sanguineri's now young man's voice says. 'How many ages hence shall our lofty scene be acted in states unborn and accents yet unknown?"

Like Indianapolis, the song *Say a Little Prayer for You* will be applicable.

He first picks up his luggage and then meets his waiting contact.

They do not need to take the shuttle to long term parking, but rather walk across the concourse's driveway into short term parking. Then they take the long ride into Sacramento.

From there they execute a recon route circling every direction where events are to be finalized for the one who does not know Sanguineri's ritual operation is to be performed.

Accommodations for this event are frugal. A Motel 6 room on 30th Street was reserved for Sanguineri. It does not bother him. Better than the days he learned his trade and many times applied afterward.

Restaurants are nearby, a grocery store and plenty of places with drive-up take out. The leaders of each team meet in his room, eat and discuss logistics.

The Sisters of Mercy, as they call themselves, run Mercy Hospital on the corner of 40th and J streets in the district called east Sacramento.

Across the street on the corner of 39th and J is Sacred Heart Church. The rectory is behind with an entrance down 39th.

Around 1952 they built a new pediatric hospital there, and broke from Church teachings and traditions and lost their way to Lucifer who demands sacrifice. Such things have become termed the Standard of Care.

If not medical and a false religious excuse, they would be imprisoned for child molestation.

Interesting how sometimes nuns travel pairs. It does seem to be a girl thing.

Again, in the early evening after a full day's work where some help molest children, two leave the hospital across 39th street on the same side as Sacred Heart. It is just a mater of driving to where they are walking and a double tapping visited each nun.

This was a two-for-one and a bag was tossed.

The immediate exit route is in a quiet residential area three blocks long and no cross streets. They speed at first and slow at the first stop sign.

Making it to a 65th Street shopping Mall they change vehicles.

For extra security another vehicle transfer is executed twenty miles away in the town of Davis.

Sanguineri remembers a teaching of Sun Tzu 'Attack when the opponent is unprepared and appear where least expected.'

This is an unwritten motto for these who have been visited by Sanguineri.

Sanguineri sits living air travel his usual way.

Flying and using his mind constructively is a safer way to exhibit repetitive behavior.

Better than taking the same route to work, shopping on a schedule in stores of familiarity, getting fast food from the same drive-throughs closest to home, and just about everything else people do in their lives.

While in the heavens *Let It Be* comes to mind.

The unknown Chief Agent and the two agents previously with bhim are gathered with others seated around a large circular desk.

The Chief Agent informs them Sanguineri is headed back to Boston.

Agent 1, "As you know the news of this has gone national. Everyone is clamoring. Fear is gripping the medical professions. Even their Washington and State lobbyists are demanding a resolution. Political contributions are at stake."

Agent 2. "Paranoia is gipping the ranks everywhere."

Chief Agent, "Deploy security immediately."

"I, Satan, accuse you of not giving proper respect to the most Holy-Almighty.

This leads to your disrespectful actions to the nature of your own lives as well as to the lives entrusted in your care.

You stand on delusional ramparts boasting over the most Holy-Almighty. You think your relationship worthy with the most Holy-Almighty. This is not so,

Your humanity is peculiarly uncouth."

PARENTING

Sanguineri says, "We are created for a purpose. The mother brings forth life. She is the focus of creation and nature.

She must stay faithful in the way she makes inside her.

The most Holy-Almighty made the mother to be the initial force for humanity leading a life that is true.

She is to be a bright lighthouse beacon shining.

The mother must never waiver."

Before Dominic, Leo and Angela have their conference with Dr. Williams and Chief Kenny they decide to go to lunch.

The eatery is close to work.

Dominic, out of habit directs the two to a back table where he can look at those coming and going.

After receiving the next big choice in life is what to order.

The waitress figuring they had enough time to decide their culinary fate approaches, "Decided yet?"

Leo orders last, then excuses himself.

Immediately Angela leans forward and says to Dominic, "You guys go further back. Both of you are not willing to admit it. Fess up quick or I'll pester ya to death like a slow dripping faucet."

Dominic smiling with a chuckle responds, "When I was 16, I left home, moved to Rome, and became what people call a 'Starving Artist.' "

Angela, "Well?"

Dominic getting the gist she is learning the technique continues, "His father was sitting at an open café where we met. He offered me help. So, he ordered the best Five Knuckle Sandwich any great Italian chef would be proud to serve up. Impressive – truly impressive. He was fast."

Then Angela continued their game, "Aaaand?"

Dominic finished with, "He changed my life. We got to know one another. He helped me move here to Boston. I lived with some distant relatives working my way through college studying Criminal Justice of all things. Did my stint with the Corps and finished in the reserves. The rest is history.

Angela somewhat confused answers, "So Leo is doing the same thing with the reserves. I thought his father worked in Thailand."

Dominic, "He was a Lifer in the Corps, talented enough to earn a few gigs at an Embassy. Did criminal justice and international relations to keep busy and was ready to move on when he retired."

Angela, "This is like one big happy family."

Dominic, "We are all Lifers in one way or another. Analyze if you want. We know our destiny is with one another."

Angela, "What's a Lifer."

Dominic laughing, "Lazy Inefficient Fool Expecting Retirement."

Angels, "Where are his parents now?"

Dominic, "They're close by. Sometimes."

Leo returns and the waitress brings their orders. Angela could not resist and jokingly tells Leo she heard he was a Lifer.

Leo responds, with a glare at Dominic realizing he had been had, "Sure am. Sometimes I think that during the life it should end with Escaping Reality,"

The waitress brings their orders and they start eating lunch.

Feeling trapped Leo finishes lunch first and says, "Almost time to meet with Chief."

Dominic, "OK. We'll get there."

Leo pays for everyone's lunch and returns waiting for them to finish. In the meantime, he has more coffee.

When they are leaving Angela projects, "I hope the meeting will find some answers about that killer."

The three then return to their eventual meeting with Chief Kenny and Dr. Williams.

Chief Kenny walks in while the three are beginning to take a seat saying, "We're meeting with Dr. Williams early."

Dominic and Leo grab their files and notebooks, and follow their Chief.

Angela follows them back to her office she where she worked for Dr. Williams.

All seems a ritual.

After passing through Charlene's rare somber attitude, the group enters Dr. William's office.

Dr. Williams starts by telling them they had received the killer's initial profile from the FBI.

Dominic and Leo put their material next to their seats and keep their notebooks to record tidbits of information.

Dr. Williams states they have correctly summed the basic indicators in the profile the FBI's Behavioral Science just sent them.

Dr. Williams, "Yes, the killer is likely to be trained and skilled. He also might have had a long military history. Also, he may have had some experience with any number of covert governmental and -or private agencies. He is not alone. He has at least one partner, though the FBI is thinking more along the lines there is group activity."

Angela then discusses. "As we all know the victims are all women. The thinking is he is highly misogynistic. It stems from either a bad mother relationship, a severe traumatic event with a woman during childhood, or both to varying degrees. Even one single event can scar a lifetime. His inner child has been psychologically destroyed to a point where he can never recover."

Chief Kenny adds, "Dr. Alverado was right on target with the cosmetic rep. The pig with a golden ring in its snout pertains to a beautiful woman who shows no discretion."

Next Dr. Williams educated the three police officers, "The first tokens left are indicators of the Great Mother Goddess. They are the three transformations in the real life of a woman and common worldwide mythology. It is what Jung called the Collective Unconscious."

Leo interrupts, "How spooky is this gonna get?"

Angela continues from Dr. Williams, "San Francisco's crescent moon is the Maiden, the young lady of springtime. Seattle's full moon symbolizes the Mother who brings life. St. Louis's reddish-brown is an eclipse. This one is the ancient wise Woman, crone, hag, and witch, with blood power, magic and knowledge kept inside. The other two naturally shed blood."

Chief Kenny informs the group, "New to us is the two Sacramento Nuns bag had a sea dragon token. The fact two were killed could have been coincidence of being together and represent the same evil to him. This is where we know he is working with others. A witness saw him leave in a car driven by another man. It may also explain his financing."

Dr. Williams, "Sea dragons are related to seahorses. The object of the attack is what one single person represented."

Angela further relates, "these zootypes are psychic archetypes. The moon tokens are similar. They represent basic feminine nature symbolic to life. These are primal gods. They do not outwardly represent basic gods present in human or semi-human form though the symbolism is now hidden."

Leo, "Zootypes?"

Angela, "Yes, total animal form not combined with a body part. Like a South American jaguar god."

Dr. Williams, "This guy knows his stuff. Outside biblical knowledge he knows ancient religions.

Dr. Williams continues by telling the others he will bring in some books by related to this matter from his personal library.

After continued discussion Chief Kenny, Dominic and Leo depart.

Dr. Williams and Angela then review psychological conditions and disorders that might relate to the killer. They also look into types of team predation.

When Angela is leaving, she looks at Charlene and says, "You're right, you've been right all along. There's a chemical axiom: Like Dissolves Like."

Charlene, "Women often get men to do the dirty work for them."

Angela, "Take out the garbage,"

Charlene, "That's why they have sex therapy and anger management."

Angela, "They'll always have work in our generation."

Charlene, "Women cheat more than men. They justify it as growing apart or wanting to find themselves. Yet they will always find a way to blame and destroy the man with rumors. Often, they drive the man away."

Angels, "It's now the national pastime in movies and commercials to make men idiots."

Charlene replies, "Some fantasies are healthy, others need healing."

Angela, "Whatever will happen if this goes public beyond the medical community is very scary. Copycats might abound."

Charlene changes the subject, "I think for now it would be best to back off the personal level. Give Breathing room. See what happens over time."

There has been a lull in reported activity, until:

In late another September the New England Urological Association's annual meeting with continuing education units is being held at Disney's Swan Hotel far away Orlando. Restaurants and lounges, many specialty and gift stores, and a Mandara spa are all available.

Nice place for a tax-deductible vacation.

The one sent follows a doctor with a distinguished look on his face leaving a lecture room alone.

He walks angrily toward the elevator.

Sanguineri, dressed as a priest skips once to keep up. The doctor presses the elevator button.

The door opens and they enter. Inside the elevator the doctor presses one of the top floor buttons and Sanguineri presses the button for the floor that exits one story earlier.

Soft canned music plays.

Sanguineri asks, "You belong to the meeting?"

Dr., "Yes Father. But sadly no. They couldn't handle my lecture. Children suffer American ways,"

Sanguineri, "What do you mean? That convention is not quite my specialty."

Dr., "They're urologists. I'm a pediatric urologist. Almost my entire practice fixes their surgical mistakes from all fields of medicine. Pediatricians and OBGYN mostly. They're savages. An incidence is malpractice, but the procedure is abuse. Their hearts are hard."

Sanguineri, "In a way I can understand that. Psychologists teach anatomy is destiny. Destroy known God given anatomy and the creation is a tortured soul."

Dr., "There are about 200 deaths a year in the US. There are about 4% reportable errors for the procedure. Reportable errors are those in the operating room. After that they are not reportable. And there way more than 10% complications for one complication alone. Improper development is wide and then considered normal."

Sanguineri, "Lucky they don't remember."

Dr., "Facts don't cease because they are ignored."

Sanguineri, "Once you give up your integrity the rest is a piece of cake."

Dr., "They think they're immune from those national killings."

Sanguineri, "I understand suffering in silence."

Dr., "God save us all."

Sanguineri, "For some, God already has."

Leaving the encounter Sanguineri adds, "We can only try to do our best with the talents god gave us."

Sanguineri returns to the Hotel's ground floor where two urologists pass him."

First urologist is saying, "Can you imagine that Pediatric Urologist telling us we shouldn't do that?"

Second urologist, "Them and a lot of the doulas, with nine months of for nearly nothing it's a quick buck especially for the OBGYNS."

First urologist, "What's the complaint. We often refer to the pediatrician."

Second Urologist, "Later, I'm going to the head."

Sanguineri knows his mission and follows the second urologist into the bathroom. He takes out his cell phone, hits the pre-arranged number and says, "One of the proper targets has been acquired, be ready."

He enters the bathroom using his elbow to open the door. Sanguineri observes the Urologist going into a stall and one man leaving after washing his hands.

Next, he takes out a pair of light surgical gloves, puts them on and moves the sign outside entry that says the bathroom saying it is being cleaned.

Then he enters the stall next to the urologist, shuts the door, pulls out a toilet seat cover and puts it on the toilet seat.

He turns and looks through the door's little side space and sees not on else has entered.

Moving around with feet facing door he bends down looking through the lower space to see if the urologist is sitting in the proper position.

He turns facing the toilet, loudly takes some toilet paper from the roll in the dispenser, puts it in the toilet, pulls out his gun and hops on top of the toilet seat.

Rising to a standing position he balances with one hand on the top of the stall, kicks the flush, reaches over and double taps the urologist.

Stepping down he slides the paper bag into the urologist's stall while observing the body and blood flow.

He puts his gun in its holster under his priest's coat, peeks out rechecking and sees still no one coming in, opens the stall.

So, he opens the stall door with his gloved hand and leaves. He turns with his back to the main lobby, looks at the sign keeping it in its place, takes off his gloves.

Sanguineri takes his time through the lobby, leaves and looks for the vehicle waiting for him.

Outside Sanguineri thinks to himself in a more adult voice, 'Many terrible things are done with the excuse that progress requires them, but they are not really required at all, just terrible things.'

His ride is at the front in the Swan Hotel's circular driveway. He briskly goes to it and enters the back seat. Inside is the driver, a front passenger while another is in the back with him.

A change of clothes awaits. His priestly garments are stuffed in a duffle bag.

There's silence as Sanguineri changes clothes. A few miles away they meet their transfer vehicle.

Once in, Sanguineri states, "I told you this would not be good. Surveillance has me. I don't think the disguise was good enough to fool facial recognition. If they run it and some computer geek may put it together.

They reassure him.

After changing in the new vehicle Sanguineri is given a preliminary packet. The driver informs him, "They've walked it through and are ready."

Departing Miami, he thinks the song: *I'll Be Seeing You*.

Boston is a great place for the most Holy-Almighty's purpose. This is especially true during the later and earlier parts of the year. People venture less. It is crowded enough to get lost and open enough due to its transportation avenues to get away.

The purge has returned.

Narcissistic people in their image of God tent to be open gravitating to degrees of flamboyance. In tribal environments there is a tendency for unit rewarding.

This gives Sanguineri a treasure of options.

The old environment is autumn and a rainy late afternoon. People have usually arrived home from work.

At a distance from the entrance to the Butcherie a man stands in a recess with an umbrella.

Every now and then someone walks by.

A bearded man leaves the Butcherie with a couple of bags under his arm. He hurries under the rain. The man of meaning is not perceived.

As the shopper gets closer to his parked car across the street and down the road from the Butcherie the man can't be seen.

When the bearded one is opening his car Sanguineri says, "Rabbi, let me help you."

The Rabbi concentrating on getting the bags in his car says to Sanguineri, "Thank you so very much."

Once seated properly before putting his keys in the ignition and as starting his automobile he turns to face to Sanguineri with a continuing smile   of gratitude ready to give one sent more salutations.

But it's too late. His greeter to that which lies beyond is in motion and shoots the Rabbi.

Gloved Sanguineri pushes the Rabbi where he falls on the seat toward the passenger door where he slumps down and would be out of site until the weather clears.

Immediately after quietly double tapped his target the paper bag with its unique content is thrown in and Sanguineri shuts the driver's door.

It is all well and good that the rain heaven sent is falling hard. People will be looking down, with covered heads for protection from nature's refreshment.

This helped before in Seattle.

Leaving the Rabbi in the fresh tomb of his enclosed car was only a matter of efficiency.

A team member in one of the prearranged escape vehicles drives up to him with a brief stop for Sanguineri to get in and onward ever onward.

How sweet it is. Like clockwork catching by surprise those studying and trying to apprehend him with his change in Victimology.

The clock is ticking. Its hands are moving. Time id of the essence.

Sanguineri now in a man's warrior voice thinks, 'Why do people play killing games on children? Reality is such behavior as theirs is that the individual is not a killer, but the group is. Bu identifying with the group, the individual transforms into a killer.'

"I, Satan, accuse you of your unfaithfulness to the most Holy-Almighty.

The result is to lead astray all who come after you into untruthful existence.

You have taken the one grand gesture of your enemy. This led to mating her identity as a bridegroom in blood, anathema to the most Holy-Almighty.

The result is that you do not defend your flock, but lead them to slaughter.

Cease, or one allowed will surely visit you."

Maturing

"I, Satan, tell you in no uncertain terms you are on the road to oblivion.

The child is brought forth from the mother. Children extend continuance. They are the focal purpose of creation and new beginnings.

People must remain steadfast toward the nature intended in their creation.

The most Holy-Almighty made children to be everlasting recyclers for humanity leading a life true.

Society's adults must be strong, maintain and act with resolve to say so. The child must never be altered."

Teams are efficient. Terrain studied. Location determined. Movements planned. Timing perfected.

After visiting the Rabbi, it doesn't take much time to reach Boston's Holy Cross Cathedral.

For repentance Sanguineri only needed a dry overcoat and clean socks.

Absolution may be a problem.

During this brief intermission he philosophizes. 'It is the child that ultimately judges.'

After being let out of the car on Washington Street in front of the Cathedral, Sanguineri climbs the steps entering the inner vestibular area through the right-side set of two large wooden doors.

He stops at a bowl of holy water, dips in two fingers of his right hand, makes the Sign of the Cross, and enters.

The sight is stunning, actually beautiful. It is about one hundred yards long with a main walkway down the center and two walkways less wide to each side for people to find the pew of their choice to sit on. Next to the side aisles are tall arching columns supporting a height of one hundred and twenty feet.

The Cathedral is ninety feet wide. Walls possess exquisite stained glass windows exhibiting themes as light passes through.

Far inside at the end from the vestibule's entryway is the altar. In front is the communion rail. Behind the altar reside the tools of mystery in a castle unto itself.

He finds the nave at the side and pensively lights a candle for the souls 100,000 who cry to the Lord in their bloodstained robes, as well as those he dispatched from the living.

From praying he locates where confessions are being heard. Taking a seat away from those waiting their turn he rests.

Mulling over his sins was eternity. Sanguineri is not the accuser. He is not the one who holds court and decides. He is not the jury.

Those he has visited are not even his peers.

Speculations and thoughts that extend have been written about, discussed and debated for millennia.

What is the purpose of his life? It is known we are all here for the purpose of helping others. So, why is he casting stones? He knows because he cannot feel.

Sanguineri made sure he would be the last. He does not know how long this would take. Negotiation brings many things unforeseen.

The little light over the priest's entrance turned on indicating the priest was ready to hear his confession.

Slowly, in deep thought, he walks to the confessional and enters. After sitting, the little sliding door opens. Sanguineri says in a low voice through the screened opening. "Bless me father for I have sinned."

The priest's indistinct face hearing confession glides in close with his ear directed toward Sanguineri.

The priest asks, "What is it my son?"

Two noise suppresser shots are barely heard by this one allowed. Who knows if the priest heard them? It does not matter.

The priest lost his Morning Star. He ceased to hear the message of the one sent who spoke through the Spirit most Holy about her creation millennia ago.

To confirm his kill, he takes out a knife and a flashlight especially for this occasion. He rips the screen and shines the light to locate his non-moving target.

To make sure he double-taps the priest again.

Then he phones his contact.

Sanguineri shoves his token bag through the screen's opening thinking, 'People read, preach and wait for the great demon to come in the end days; but they should look into themselves for the answer.'

With a sigh Sanguineri leaves the confessional.

Walking out the center main aisle he hums slightly aloud the song: *My Way*.

Outside the heavy pouring rain has become an overcast drizzle.

He notices the streets are cleaner.

His ride pulls up. They leave.

Sanguineri's internal adult voice derides, 'Forgiveness is their code. But there is no forgiveness in denying the spirit most Holy.'

Domonic is notified a priest has been executed and a bag was founf. He first tells Leo then Chief Kenny.

Kenny says he will tell Angela and Dr. Williams.

They rust to Holy Cross Cathedral where all has been secured.

There are extraordinary numbers of bystanders with the press. Cameras and crews.

In the vestibule they find the Officer in Charge Grant, who tells them a nun found the priest's body.

Dominic requests to see her and Officer Grant has Officer Polk take them to her.

After polite introductions Dominic asks, "Sister, would you please tell us what you know. We realize you are repeating yourself but we would appreciate hearing it first-hand."

Sister Magdalena re-tellingly states, "Yes, I understand. I began my work at the nave cleaning and placing new candles. When I finished with that, I noticed one of the doors open at the confessional. Confessions were over so I went to see. I checked out the open door and saw the screen had been torn. Then I went inside and looked through the screen. This is when I saw father. It was horrible. I rushed to tell Monsignor. He phoned 911 and reported it to the police.

Dominic finishes taking notes of the nun's statement.

He thanked Sister Magdalena and gives her his card requesting she contact him if anything else comes to mind.

She responds, "Certainly detective Alighieri. Your name will be easy to remember,"

Dominic, "Yours too Sister."

Leo asks Officer Polk about photography.

Officer Polk points to the direction of the confessional and tells them how to get there.

Joe sees them coming. When they are close enough to hear him, Joe states, "Hell's officially open."

Leo inquires, "What do you mean?"

Danny, "Remember the doctor killings? We got this other bag. Take a look. We notified Chief Kenny immediately. That's probably why you're here."

Dominic looks at the priest in eternal slumber.

Leo is now doing his quick exam, "Up close and personal. Two are by his ear. One probably would not have been fatal. There might others but his head is too blown out gory. We'll wait for the coroner."

Danny excuses himself and Joe, "We're done here."

Leo, "Good, the coroner should be here soon."

The coroner finally arrives and starts marking on her body sketch pad.

With her hands in gloves, she turns the priest's head showing Leo.

She indicates, "There are four entry points. The exits made a mess."

Then the coroner motions the back wall describing, "There are blood splatters around here that appear consistent with the shooting."

Leo, "Looks like one round is lodged here in the wall opposite the screen."

The coroner finally states "I'm going to take the body now."

Crime Kit Officer, Johnson, in the confessional where Sanguineri sat ponders, "Let's see if we can get any fingerprints."

Dominic, "You'll find a million."

The two homicide detectives return to Officer Grant.

Grant informs them, "Monsignor is waiting."

Again, Grant has Polk take them to the next interview, Monsignor Hart.

They exchanged greetings preparing their notebooks for this on-site statement.

But Dominic receives a phone call from Chief Kenny notifying the Rabbi has been found and about a meeting he wants a meeting the day.

Dominic makes the interview purposely short and thanks the Monsignor telling him about the Rabbi.

Monsignor Hart understands. They agree to meet later with Chief Kenny.

The evenings are getting longer. By this time families have finished dinner.

They proceed to the Rabbi's just reward.

While on their way, Dominic observes, "His timing is perfect. This is more than coincidence."

Leo, "We know it's not random. He kills only who he has set out to kill."

Dominic, "Not quite a 'kill them all' thing.

Leo, "It's a deep pit we are looking into."

Dominic, "We may be in for another night like we had with the doctors."

Leo, "Yep. A definite maybe."

Dominic, "We're not prepared. Never thought this guy would come back to haunt us."

Leo recounts, "Remember the cosmetics rep? She was politically connected."

Dominic, "Right invariably become abridged as despotism increases. Whatever profession the despotism involves."

Leo, "Question authority: authority increases violence to maintain itself. He's not questioning."

Reaching the Rabbi they see Officer Jackson and the unit from Sanguineri's previous encounters.

Checking in with Officer Jackson, Jackson tells them, "When Kenny learned about the priest's bag he got team together again."

Continuing Jackson hands Dominic his notes, "Here's the preliminary."

Dominic stays with Jackson while Leo walks to the coroner's assistant handling this call. He looks inside and asks, "what are your findings."

Coroner, "Two head wounds. Body temp says he's been here for hours."

Leo circles the Rabbi's car noticing the team covered all bases.

He and Lincoln exchange nods. Lincoln tells Leo his findings.

Leo returns to the Rabbi's driver's side now open door, and peers in to confirm the bag's presence. He notes to himself how similar most crimes have been.

Arriving back to Dominic and Jackson, Leo says, "Out in the open during the day and he got close to both the priest and Rabbi."

Jackson, "Madison questioned people at the Butcherie. They said it was raining hard. Nobody saw or heard a thing."

Dominic, "He used the weather as cover."

Leo, "Windows are up with no holes. Linclol said there seems to be no stray bullet marks and most everything is litter."

Dominic, "Photography?"

Jackson, "They took the Cathedral photos and are on their way,"

Chief Kenny phoned Dominic reminding him about the meeting with others present.

Dominic mentions bringing something for everyone to eat during the conference. With notebook at the ready Dominic waits for Chief Kenny to get the menus desired.

Chief Kenny tells Dominic that he will get the fixings and have coffee ready.

Dominic, "Thanks Chief. Deep within your pompous exterior there beats a heart of true kindness."

Eating can become a serious endeavor. Often it evolves to ritualistic behavior. It is a wonder these two investigators have not become too heavy.

The morning meeting with Dr. Williams's is now in a larger conference room with a couple of Crime Boards and victim pictures.

Chief Kenny announces, "We're staying alert with presence on the streets the next few nights."

Introduction, including Lau, were exchanged.

Lau, from regional intelligence center, was busy updating as information comes in.

Dr. Williams, "The doctors are secondary now. We need to find roots."

Angela, "Partly it's how the perpetrator feels about his victims. He considers them guilty."

Kenny, "A man has two reasons for what he does – the one that sounds good and the real one."

Dr. Williams, "The human race has a long history of hurting each other."

Angela, "All these doctors had malpractice claims for similar surgeries. He really feels he's punishing people who hurt others."

Kenny, "Now the victims are different."

Angela, "Religion and sexual mania are closely related. We're dealing with death cult stuff."

Dr. Williams, "These are crimes of passion, not profit."

Angela, "The game that both sides must be saying to their victims is that: Without their death, their pain, without the sacrifice, they would be nothing."

Kenny, "They kill them because they believe, or maybe because the victims are taught to believe."

Dr. Williams, "Both are reasons enough. It comes from early childhood experience. We only know as adults what we feel as children. We are probably dealing with a form of societal Repetition Compulsion in the victims,"

Continuing, Dr. Williams continues, "The deaths are in ritual. They are play deaths. All ritual had a death component, then the victim reemerges a new person."

Angela, "All cruelty stems from weakness."

Charlene peeks in, "Monsignor Hart and Rabbi Cohen are here. Imam Samouni has a meeting."

All stand and exchange greetings.

Monsignor puts some bags of the desk, "We've brought some food for everyone to munch on."

Rabbi Cohen puts his bags on the desk at the same time, "We also have drinks."

Food is great for International Relations. It is where people meet.

Rituals grow; and usually have feasts.

Kenny, "We need you help with the token list I sent you."

Rabbi Cohen, "Monsignor and I have talked and agree to bring our Testaments."

Monsignor, "Your analysis of the first three is correct. The moon ornaments are its theological three stages. They link worldwide usage to the ancient feminine. This is short notice so forgive us if we are incomplete."

Rabbi Choen, "These moon symbols are even Judeo-Christian with New, Full and the eclipsing moon. The nurse's is the biblical screech owl of the wilderness. It represents Lilith. Lilith was the female demon that attacked children and a certain body part. Her origins were in Mesopotamia as a minor wind spirit.

Rabbi Cohen continued, "You were also correct about the swine with a gold ring in its snout. Swine are feminine fertility symbols from Melanesia to Greece. It is the most prolific farm animal. When mated with more than one boar the sow has an average of two or more piglets in her litter."

Monsignor, "The Cardiologist's hippopotamus is an icon for the Great Mother goddess in the waters. It stems from inland Africa."

Rabbi, "The OBGYN's stingray with the stinger painted red is that the stinger was the main cutting instrument in Mayan bloodletting rituals. The male's blood was collected and spread on the ground to fertilize the Great Mother Earth goddess to ensure a good harvest. Only women could bleed the men and only the king's mother or wife could bleed him."

Monsignor, "The pediatrician's crocodile is an Egyptian totem similar to the hippopotamus."

Rabbi, "Baton Rouge's little bird may be a swallow or a sparrow where both carry curses."

Monsignor, "The Brocton bear and the Winter Haven's cow are earth symbols of rebirth and regeneration. Bears hibernate in winter and mothers, in rebirth, come out of their den with cubs. Cow skulls are the female reproductive tract. "

Rabbi, "The Miami turtle can have two meanings. In Japan the earth rests on the Great Mother's shell. In the Philippines, the turtle tricks the monkey."

Kenny, "The Miami doctor was Filipina."

Monsignor, "The nun's sea dragon is the ancient Mesopotamian Leviathan, the feminine force that lives in the seas. She evolved into the biblical dragon the Harlot rides on in Revelation."

Rabbi, "The Indianapolis cat is to the feminine, and the Urologist's boar is another pig fertility symbol."

Chief Kemmy, "The token left at the crime scenes of today's killings are both frogs. Please tell us about frogs."

Rabbi, "Frogs are early in the Moses Pharaoh confrontation. They come after the Nile turned red. Red represents blood and frogs the offspring from the bloody waters. Blood and water are mythic feminine."

Monsignor, "In Revelation there are three frogs that came out of the mouth of the beast and spew blasphemy. They were in the priest and Rabbi's bags.

Dominic immediately aske, "There are three frogs?"

Monsignor, "Yes."

Chief Kenny, "There's going to be another killing. You and Dominic will be on the streets. I'll alert Jackson's crew."

After the three officers leave, the other four stay discussing biblical references, ancient mythology, the psychology of archetypes, and Lao on Sanguineri's movements.

"I, Satan, accuse you of falling away from the truth given you by the one most Holy ratified by the one most Almighty.

You have regressed into the blasphemy from which you had to leave from denying your very creation.

Your shepherdess did not seek the one lost sheep. She sought and found evil with chaos. She returned with that evil to spread her disease to the other ninety-nine.

Often the less there is to justify a tradition, the harder it is to get rid of it.

Evil has taken root within you. Rights are meaningless unless enforced.

Desist, one allowed will surely visit you."

AGING

"I, Satan, tells you that the father is brought forth with the purpose of maintaining creation's balance.

Fathers are pivot, not the totality, of which each distinct part of creation's cycle revolves.

He must remain secure for the myriad different natures intended by creation.

The most Holy made the father the supporter, provider and servant for her creation with those which he is a part, so humanity leads life that is true.

He is given power and control by the most Holy to act for behest of all. The father must not destroy.

And the one who creates him and gives him power must not destroy any part of him."

The Chief Agent is no longer in his official office, walking along concrete pathways of guarded grounds or even in an elegant conference room.

He stands in a hotel room with his two Agents.

On the phone he can be heard asking, "Are the security teams finished preparing their objectives?"

When finished he hangs up.

Agent 1 asks, "Then all set?"

Chief Agent, "Providing nothing changes."

Agent 2, "This can get touchy."

Chief Agent, "Stay confident. We're prepared."

Agent 1, "I know he wants it done. We go along. It may be good, an opportunity. But it is out of the ordinary."

Agent 2. "Do we go to our assignments now?"

Chief Agent, "Yes, I will monitor here and join you later."

The Hilton Hotel in Dedham is close to major highways in the greater Boston community. This drive took about twenty minutes from the Cathedral.

It has a restaurant, Starbucks Café, business center, full-service fitness center, indoor pool, racquetball court and tennis court. Some rooms have a Jacuzzi. The few cathedral ceilings add a nice touch.

Potential killing zones are virtually available from many rooms featuring balconies.

The Corner Suit overlooks a trail for those who appreciate nature and wish private conversation.

The Parlor suite accommodates a view of the gazebo and water fountain.

They present the best two options for an occasion such as the one now in progress. The Greater Boston Interfaith Organization is holding a meeting.

The forward element reserved both rooms for the main event as well as several other rooms them. The place for a rally after the meeting had not yet been finalized. The escape plan featured three exit routes.

All reserved rooms were set for continual monitoring.

When Sanguineri nears the hotel, he repeats in his mind something he has noticed about human behavior: 'Blind faith defies all logic.'

Upon arrival the transport team goes to the restaurant to have their evening meal.

Sanguineri leaves them for a room where logistics and supply are headquartered,

His meal awaits him.

He is experienced. Experience is learning from one's own mistakes. History is learning from other people's mistakes.

Success is on one side of a respective coin. With experience and learning Sanguineri makes ready.

All is foreseen. But both rooms are prepared though the Parlor room is according to the meeting.

Science and technology have come a long way since he first trained and worked using all progressions.

He hopes there will be a time when science and technology will overcome ignorance and superstition.

Security cameras were taken care of. Visual but no recording.

The backup firearm has been chosen over a bulky 50 caliber weapon because the distance is too close and escape would be too complicated.

This is a fine tool outfitted with a noise suppressor, spark arrester and a scope.

The reliable AK74U is also much smaller and transportable.

He has already been to a range and doped the sight to his way.

He and his spotter move the two end tables from the sides of the bed. One end table is to set the tripod at the end of the muzzle, and the other to rest his arms.

They wait with balcony door slightly open and drapes closed to a line-of-fire.

All goes according to plan. So, put the cross hairs on the target, shift position to relaxation, control breath and only apply necessary trigger pressure, do not squint.

The Imam falls in the fountain's waters.

The team immediately exits the Parlor Room.

Part of the team move to the Corner Room.

Others take the weapon, over shirt, and Handy Wipes Sanguineri used to remove powder residue from his hands, though he was gloved. They take these items to the fourth-floor armory to disassemble it.

Sanguineri exits the hotel to his awaiting transportation.

A transportation team member drops the token bag when leaving.

To the trilogy of this evening's encounters Sanguineri reflects on these victims shared misbegotten sanctified violence. 'Hate gives meaning to an otherwise meaningless life. Some of their hate hides in expressions of love.'

He now questions, 'What do you do to the taker of an eye when the taker has had his eye taken?'

Finding there will be a third termination came too late for those in Dr. Williams's meeting.

Officer Jackson's crew immediately responds when notified by Dispatch.

The detectives arrive to a crime scene full of bystanders, potential witnesses and more press than any investigator would want to deal with.

Anger and discontent permeate the situation.

Eventually, they find a place to park.

Dominic and Leo meet Jackson.

Leo asks, "Another bag?"

Jackson while giving Dominic a copy of his preliminary notes replies, "Yes. We notified Kenny who was in a meeting with Dr. Williams. Chief told us to open it and there's another frog."

Dominic, "We can't leave any stone unturned."

Jackson, "Photography is almost finished. The coroner's people are here. And, we've contacted hotel security."

Leo, "Morons have committed murder so shrewdly that it's taken over a hundred police minds to catch them. I'll check the body."

Dominic does a few quick interviews Jackson told him about. Some are family and other clergy.

He tells each they should give a more complete statement at the station sometime soon.

Lastly, Dominic meets with Imam Samouni.

When Leo finished with the body of the dispatched Imam, he returned to Dominic who asks, "Can you see the wind?"

Leo smiles replying "Let's discover what's in the wind."

Dominic, "And what this wind is."

Angela arrives at the crime scene in a squad car.

She finds Dominic and Leo.

Angela explains, "When Chief Kenny received the news of the token, he and Dr. Williams wanted me to be with you the remainder of the evening."

They ritually get coffee and munchies at the Starbuck's Café and return to Dominic's car to leave the commotion and talk things over.

When they reach the car, Dominic notices a paper bag on the ground next to his door. It is opened so the contents can be seen.

In the bag are prepaid cellular burner go-phones with a number on a sticky note held by a rubber band.

A note stapled to the bag warned Dominic they are being watched, not to contact anyone unless told to do so, and he prepared to use each phone in numbered order.

It's getting late. The action-packed game of Tag seems like an opportunity, but irksome to the trio.

They question why he wants to do this because it is so much out of his standard MO.

It couldn't be because of their winning personalities.

Also wondered, where this game of Cat and Mouse will take them.

Leo returns to Officer Davis asking him to tell Jackson they will be leaving. Officer Davis in his Southern way affirms he will tell Jackson and does so.

When Leo gets back, Dominic was on the first go-phone with Sanguineri who instructs them to go to the Paul Revere house where a bag will be waiting for them with instructions inside.

Dominic says, "So, do you plan on announcing something."

Sanguineri, "Killing them is a statement, just as those who play-kill children have their statement. I plan to be an omen for the future of others that will follow."

Dominic replies, "No book can be written to justify your behavior."

Sanguineri retorts, "It is written. I just utilize a more efficient and humane way of stoning. It's time for you three to go. Remember, you are being watched. Do not draw your weapons. Kenny and Dr. Williams are still meeting.'

While Dominic drives Leo wonders, "I would like to know where he gets his weapons."

Angela, "What society does to children, children do to society. Each in their own particular way. This is getting more and more involved as we go."

Dominic, "As it was said: Injustice anywhere is injustice everywhere. This guy is making a program of his feelings of injustice."

Angela, "A new special order against an older social program."

Leo, "In wars of ideas, people get killed."

During his wait Sanguineri tells his victims, "Children need to grow up in safety from adulthood games. They did not survive the adult games you forced upon them. So, I speak for them."

They reach the grey painted Paul Revere House with lattice covered windows.

Leo gets out. He finds a piece of paper held down by a large white stone. On the sidewalk next to the streetlight.

Leo returns. The next go-phone rings.

Dominic answers, Sanguineri says, "The visions they glorify in their minds, the ideals they enthrone in their hearts, this they will build their lives by. This they have become.

Dominic tells Sanguineri, "People with principle are always bold, but those who are bold are not always people of principle."

Sanguineri, comes back, "Tell that to those I have met. The strength and power of despotism consists wholly in the fear of resistance. But, then how can an infant strike fear? The time is coming that the infant will strike fear. In his own time."

Leo, "The note says we are to go to Paul Revere Park and there will be another note on the cement of the spiral stone structure."

Dominic to Sanguineri, "Are you the only one who appreciates your sense of humor?"

Sanguineri, "There are times when we are powerless to prevent injustice, but there should never be a time when we fail to protest."

Dominic, "Actions speak louder than words."

Sanguineri, "Actions often result in reaction. Discern the difference. It's time for you to get moving. Tell McFarland to wait a few seconds observing a five-foot perimeter around the note before he picks it up.

The trio proceeds to the next prepared objective.

Dominic, driving, says, "This has turned out to be one hell of a day."

Leo, "What did we do to deserve this guy."

Angela, "Deserve has nothing to do with it. You have been chosen."

Dominic, "Such a deal – this chosen generosity."

Sanguineri thinks deriding those he terminating, 'The next generation is theirs, and yours is ending. Your gestures are not noble."

At the spiral structure in Paul Revere Park, Leo notices three stationary little red lights and another brighter one waving. He notices one light stops and comes back on indicating the prize.

Leo returns with the note saying, "They have at least three shooters with night vision and one stronger that is not a weapon."

Dominic relates this to Sanguineri."

Sanguineri, "You have nothing to fear. It was merely to tell you we cover our bases and are ready as things may go. Contingencies."

Sanguineri next instructs them to go to the place directed in the note and specifically drive east on Boylston Street, turn left and park at Charles Street.

This will take them to Boston Commons. They are to go to the Soldiers and Sailors Monument.

Sanguineri instructed them not to draw their weapons.

The three quietly go to the next destination.

Sanguineri ponders to his victims: 'You are the evil that you think in others. The false evil you think you are curing is a sham. You have relieved your own pain by inflicting it on others."

When they reach the monument with Angela slightly behind, they are surprised to see a man waiting for them who said, "It's time we meet."

The two detectives were focused on Sanguineri; yet, Angela noticed the moving lights on their backs and then observes other lights stationary.

She moves to the front saying, "Lights are on all of us here. I'll go talk to him."

Angela continues to Dominic and Leo, "Give us some privacy."

Angela tells Sanguineri, "I'd like to ask you some questions."

Sanguineri, "That is part of the purpose we are here. Being a woman, this may not be to your liking."

Leo now turns his gaze away, looks out into the void while shrugging his shoulders saying, "I can't believe this is happening."

Sanguineri, "Dr. Alvarado you know all of you have no need to fear, but Alighieri and McFarland should be a little less on edge."

Angela slowly starts toward Sanguineri telling him, "The FBI probably know why you are doing it."

Sanguineri, "The FBI have profiled many serial killers. Of course, they know why. So does the CIA unpublished studies. You know they can't talk about it because they will lose their jobs."

Angela, "The abuse syndrome has a 'Thou Shall Not Tell' is very effective personally and socially."

Sanguineri, "The retired ones, especially those who have written their pulp books won't write about it because people will think they are raving lunatics."

Angela, "It's a very sticky wicket indeed. It's problematic if you're caught alive. They're deferring in silence regarding your actions waiting for you to drop into obscurity."

Dominic faces Leo, "Did you sense it also?"

Leo, "turns to Dominic disgustingly nodding 'yes.'

Dominic continues, "I must admit he has determined flair."

Dominic continues, "I must admit he has determined flair."

Leo, "He's not the one with an identity problem. His victims did."

Angela and Sanguineri move to Frog Pond, converse for a short period of time and then he departs.

Angela returns to her partners.

Sanguineri's ancient voice derides, "It is narcissistic to believe one belongs to a chosen way callously determining the destiny of others. The question is why I chose you."

Sanguineri melts into the immediate ether of darkness and when out of sight he hums the song *I'm So Lonesome I Could Cry.*

The next morning the two detectives arrive at work in usual fashion. Dominic made the morning's breakfast decision.

He tells Leo, "I felt like sausage biscuits, cheese, egg and hash browns. Your coffee's ready."

After moments of reflection and cuisine, Chief Kenny phones. They are to appear with their files and notebooks,

Dominic teases as if their area is bugged.

The duo enters Kenny's office where two trench-coats are waiting.

Kenny says "The FBI and CIA are here Let them see your files and notes."

The FBI Agent is facing the entrance.

A second man is standing to the side behind in the background. Dominic smiles and Leo nods.

The FBI Agent says, "We're still in charge of the case completely. He's been everywhere. And nowhere all at the same time. We will be the ones to piece it all together.

The FBI Agent reaches to take the files.

Dominic steps past him and gives the files to the second man and greets, "Semper Fi, Sir."

The second man answers back, "Semper Fi."

As Leo is walking up to the second man, the FBI Agent laughs, "Ain't Brotherly Love so precious."

Leo puts the folders into the second man's outreached and says, "Here they are dad."

Leo's father says, "Thanks, I'm here just for the visit. Chief will have the FBI's and my copies made and give the originals back to you.

Leo's father hands the files to Chief Kenny saying to Dominic and Leo, "I'll see you two later."

Chief Kenny wraps up, "You can leave now. Knuckles and the FBI will stay."

After leaving Dominic quietly says to Leo, "How much do they know? They've known him all along."

"I, Satan, accuse you of the belligerency you have become.

You have taken hate converting it into anger and use anger in improper actions of rage,

This insults the most Holy-Almighty.

Your wisdom lost the meaning of your words.

The one most Holy-Almighty has made your creation in perfection.

You bring the detested way not yours when born.

Refrain, or one allowed will surely visit you.

For, it is written."

DEATH

"I, Satan, tell you your actions lead you to predestined fated doom.

These acts are by choice causing disunity.

Your selfishness does not allow equal sharing.

Your self-created habits are destructive.

You cherish yourself doing as you please with perfect creation.

The charity you give has a price not a blessing.

You are disrespectful, unfaithful, belligerent, and have regressed into the pit.

Your social is a cycle of violence and abuse set in a game of pretend death, which is real.

The die had been cast by your ancestors.

With eyes removed, you maintain its molding in entertainment and feasting.

This essential vision was sent with him allowed.

Heed this warning, for such things will surely come to pass."

The following day everyone is attending to their respective business. Dominic and Leo sit at their desks with leftover mystery breakfast.

Leo is unusually wearing a coat and tie.

Dominic has already read the morning paper telling the previous evening's wondrous events.

Charlene phones saying: "It is I – Charlene. Dr. Williams would like both of you to come over now. Hurry, I'm having a hard time waiting."

When the two arrive Charlene, with a large smile greets them. She leaves her desk and opens the door to Dr. William's inner sanctum.

The two detectives enter. Charlene follows.

In attendance were the usual suspects:

Dr. Williams, Dr. Alvarado – Angela and Chief Kenny.

Dr. Williams tells them to, "Take a seat. You have something unexpected."

Chief Kenny informed them, "A package has arrived. It's been cleared. There appears to be a present for each of us. Lucky Charlene has two. They are heavy."

Dr. Williams distributes the presents telling, "Even Officer Jackson's team received a package."

Kenny continued, "He must have known a lot about us and what we doing every step of the way,"

Angela, "We have no idea why he picked us, or even Boston to concentrate so many of his killings."

Dominic queried, "Does it have a return address with a name.?"

Charlene, "Raphael Michaels. The packages were sent from Valentine, Nebraska,

Angela, "His message continues."

Everyone opens their package. In each one is a pair of bookends: Passionate doves looking outward:

After the first contents were revealed, Charlene opens her second present.

She exclaims, "There's a note inside. It says: 'Especially for you Charlene. Your fine sense of humor about mankind can handle its meaning."

Charlene then takes out her prize describing, "Hey look, it is a frog that has a tied red scarf around its neck with a pompom ball at each end. There is a red Christman elf hat on its head. It's soft and cuddly."

Charlene presses a button. Ther frog starts croaking Jingle Bells. They listen to its humor. Angela senses a message. Charlene lets it play through.

Dominic teasingly says, "Your frog's a real trophy. It'll remind you of all the people who croaked."

Dr. Williams quickly interjects with a serious tone, "It appears that it is much easier for people to die for their religion, than to live up to it."

Chief Kenny stops the party, "OK! Let's get back to work and finish our reports."

Reports were completed. Relief is setting in. Rest will be over the horizon.

Until – Angela arrived.

Angela, with a come-hither look, gingerly touches Leo's nose, saying, "See ya guys."

Leo questions, "It's Friday, wach-ya-doing?"

Angela, "I'm going to explore the galaxy to see if I can find an intelligent life form."

Leo eagerly responds, "Let's go."

He picks up and wiggles the flags at Dominic.

Leo continues, "Should I bring anything."

Angela looks directly at Leo smiling. "Only what you carry. Are you ready for the trials?"

Leo replies, "I'm not afraid"

Angela while straightening Leo's tie. "You should be – You should be."

Dominic takes the flag stand from Leo, wiggles it back at him, and then leans back with a smirk.

Dominic states the obvious, "Confident you are? Your parents are back." Then mockingly, "Why not get together and have them meet Angela?"

Leo gets up to leave with Angela, "Deal."

Their glances tell Dominic good-by.

Dominic gives his regards by raising a toast to them with his coffee cup, reminding Leo not to dunk his baked potato in the coffee.

Angela and Leo leave.

After they left, Dominic takes a drink then ponders aloud, "Into the valley of death."

Sanguineri's voice of ancient days explains:

"I have been an image in a vision.

It is good to be taught by one's enemies.

Who appears an enemy is not always so.

Live life in Lessons Learned and equally in Lessons Taught.

Possess malice toward none and equality for all.

Live without illusion and selfishness.

Treat others as yourself, through sanity, in your life truly given the most Holy-Almighty.

If not: Your only hope is reincarnation."

ENTOMBMENT

"I, Satan, finish this vision sent you by the most Holy-Almighty. Learn well its meaning. Fasten it securely deep in your heart's memory.

I am not the false light fallen to earth. Your many misrepresentations have confused me with yourself.

See this light's message sent from the heavens, which is partly both Holy and Almighty.

This gifted light's message sent from the heavens, which is purity both Holy and almighty.

This gifted light also shines in you. Do not let this blessing inner light continue shrouded in a created veiled Luciferian darkness.

Your behavior is a cycle of violence that only brings destruction.

The freedom of choice for oneself in taking from others as a right may bring a return demanding onto you.

This destruction escalates until a social apocalyptic must come to pass.

Such is your history - mankind."

Also, "This vision told a fate similar for you.

Do not cross the threshold to enter for food in a cafeteria of one's own choosing.

Do not partake in what does not belong to you.

135

You desire what is not yours to take. It belongs to the most Holy-Almighty your conceiver and creator.

Again, if you consume, you will discover what may at first taste sweet to the mind's tongue, but will forever burn bitter inside you by your victim's revenge.

You take part of a temple, the tent of another.

Freedom to take without consideration is not extended to you by the most Holy-Almighty.

This wrong belongs to the soul of infinite darkness that leads you into nothingness.

The scarlet Leviathan Beast of the Sea made her inner powerful presence known. She gave her power to the Harlot who rides her. The Harlot, in turns, gives the power to act outwardly as her servant – the Behemoth of the land.

She is drunk from your blood's consumption.

You took on her mantle, the shawl you wear over your shoulders in all the ways of your life.

In doing so, you stand before the birthing of creation waiting to defile nature's perfection made.

The wheel of your end time began its turning.

The wheel's center, the hub, has the meaning of this message and pathway to your demise or forever life.

The sacrifice wear ritually bloodstained white robes and cry out for their justice.

They are in the custody of the one most Holy-Almighty, a place you cannot reach.

You have received this vision.

Put these evils to rest.

The vision of your Elijah has now ended."

www.ingramcontent.com/pod-product-compliance
Lightning Source LLC
Chambersburg PA
CBHW060937120626
46557CB00003B/1030